Undiluted Grace

Craig Stasio

Detroit Ink Publishing
Detroit, Michigan USA

Copyright

Undiluted Grace

By Craig Stasio

ISBN: 978-0-9970126-1-3

Edited by Pamela Hilliard Owens, Detroit Ink Publishing

http://detroitinkpublishing.com

Cover Design by Sydnee Turner, SydGrafix Design Specialist

http://sydgrafix.com

Published by Detroit Ink Publishing

4444 2nd Avenue

Detroit MI 48226 USA

http://detroitinkpublishing.com

Foreword

Craig has poured his heart, spirit, and testimonies in their purest form into this book. His priority while writing the book was to reveal the God he's so in love with to anyone willing to listen, despite the controversy and persecution we all know accompanies the truth. *Undiluted Grace* is just that, undiluted. Nothing has been omitted for the sake of "saving face," but rather, Craig has laid his relationship with God bare before all willing to read his story. He's expressed multiple times over the course of writing it that he "wants people to know that *they* can have this radical walk with the God of the Bible and have an intimate relationship with the One who created them". Craig didn't write this book for himself or for his own glory, he could honestly care less if he sold a single copy. He wrote it for God, and with God. It's about his Father. And people getting to know what He's REALLY like. It's not by coincidence you've found a copy in your hand, and it's not a mistake if it speaks to your heart. Jesus has a way of reaching us through the most unanticipated path and that's exactly what *Undiluted Grace* is about.

-Natasha Wartell

October 2015

Preface

This manuscript is a compilation of radical and super natural life-changing personal experiences. Initially I tried to avoid writing this book knowing that its controversial content would only bring more persecution into my life. But as hard as I tried to avoid this task, the Lord only further convinced me to write the book. The final straw was a personal prayer where I told the Lord that if He really wanted ne t write this book that He needed to give me the title to it. I finished this elaborate prayer by telling Him that once He gave me the title, I would again dedicate myself to writing. That afternoon at about 3:00, a minister friend of mine met with me having no knowledge of the inner turmoil I was undergoing at the mere thought of writing a controversial book such as this one. My minister friend approached me and out of nowhere began to tell me about a vivid dream he had just had. He also emphasized the face that he felt convicted and compelled by God to share this dream with me immediately. He went in to tell me the dream:
"We were standing together in a bookstore. You were doing a book signing of a new book you had written, and the name of the book was *Undiluted Grace*."

My friend then asked me if that dream meant anything to me. As quietly as I could I excused myself from the conversation and brought my focus back to God and to His desire and command that I write this book.

The story you are about to read, while appearing to be very fictional, is nothing of the sort. The story you will soon read will undoubtedly shake you in ways I can't even begin to describe. Allow yourself an open mind, heart, and spirit as you allow me to share what can happen when a simple man embarks on a journey with a modern day God in the most practical, yet radical way I could have ever imagined.

Acknowledgements

I want to thank the people who have inspired me to complete this awesome task of writing Volume One of *Undiluted Grace*. The first and foremost person to inspire and compel me to complete this mandate was my loving and faithful wife Danielle. Her strength and passion have helped to uphold me for a decade now. The compilation of this manuscript has been very much taxing on my relationships and on my personal life. The continued encouragement from this great bride of mine has been a most powerful driving force to complete this task.

I would also like to give a heartfelt thanks to my brothers, sisters, and children who stood by me through this process offering priceless help, especially Brittany, Erica, Jaclyn, Allison, Jessie, Alaina, Leah, Natasha, and Lizzie.

Introduction

Undiluted Grace is a radical but true modern day story of another "Saul of Tarsus." This story will give you a first-hand and up close look into the mind and heart of a man hijacked by God in the most unthinkable of ways. The God of the Bible has not stopped writing stories like the ones in the Manuscript He wrote long ago. For centuries, the God of the Bible has been carrying out auditions to see if anyone would like the privilege of being a modern day character in one of His stories. This book is the result of one man's acceptance of such an invitation.

Without knowing the cost of the all-consuming effects this acceptance would have on his life, here was a man who dared to say, "Yes" to this invitation. This book is but a magnifying glass that will allow you to experience the events as they unfolded and continue to unfold. Be prepared to have your preconceived notions of Christianity and religion in general shattered. Allow yourself to again see through the eyes of a child.

The God of the Bible is about to be revealed to you in a way that many have never experienced. This book is a beacon in the darkness of the modern day church. It is a lighthouse to lead people to safety in the midst of a worldwide spiritual storm.

The Lord once said:

"Then you will know the truth and the truth will set you free."

Allow those very words to help you judge the story that is to follow.

About the Author

Craig Stasio is a minister who resides in the suburbs of Detroit, Michigan. Craig moved to the United States at the age of 18 after being raised in Sardegna, Italy. He is married to Danielle, and they are raising three wonderful children. Craig is a licensed chiropractor and business owner. Craig has left his old life behind for the chance to fulfill the dream of so many before him, that of walking the narrow road of faith.

Table of Contents

Chapter 1: The Darker Mind

Angels, demons, miracles, Heaven, Hell, and a supernatural God; these are some of the most controversial and heavily discussed topics in today's world. A relentless quest to find the smallest trace of answers to countless questions regarding such matters has left so many unsatisfied. Some have exhausted every known means possible to them on this venture; others have casually browsed through the evidence presented to them throughout their life, with little more than a shrug of the shoulders at the end. For those of you that carry an insatiable hunger within the deepest parts of your being for answers: prepare to be satisfied. The spiritual realm will no longer be a mystical distant myth, for I am about to take you on a true voyage into this unseen realm. Prepare to have preconceived notions shattered. Dare to allow yourself to see with more than just your natural eyes. Sit back, buckle up, and settle in for the ride of your life—as I will now share the story of a man, whose life was hi-jacked in a radical way, catapulting him into a reality that his heart and mind had always labeled as fiction.

Our story will begin in the autumn of 2005. Back then I was a 38-year-old man that had endured the rugged terrain of a tumultuous path I called life. I had graduated chiropractic college 10 years prior and was a successful businessman by the standards of society. I had always been one that would shoot for the stars with any venture I would set my mind to. This grandiose way of undertaking quests led me to opening several large practices throughout the suburbs where I lived. I had hired multiple doctors to participate in this game of Monopoly my life was becoming. Financially I had achieved what most suburbanites would consider a state of comfort.

(As per relationships, divorce at a young age had already left its scars on my life. Marriage had invaded my young life at the age of 26 as part of a circumstantial calamity that left a young woman without most of her family.

Without understanding of the commitment and responsibilities associated with this sacred union I married as a means of trying to help her. I realized shortly after that it was too late, that it was never love that had propelled me into marrying her. After the separation I remarried. During this marriage I became a dad to three children. At this point in my story I had been married for about 5 years.)

My life seemed to fit the perfect model that society lays out for each one of us to accomplish. Every box on the page of my life had now been checked off: a career, a family, a beautiful house, and financial stability. But tucked away inside me there was a part of me as empty as the day I came into this world. While the business and social parts of my life were flourishing beyond the expectations of many around me, they did little to satisfy a burning desire within me to know my purpose on this planet. As a child I had been gifted with an incredible mind. An affinity to navigate easily through complex math and science had catapulted me into special schools. In my early adulthood I had also became a member of the intellectual elite group called Mensa. I reasoned that this mind I had been gifted with was what propelled me to try and find real answers to swirling questions involving creation, religion, and, more than anything else, the spirit realm.

Unfortunately, as many before me, my curiosity catapulted me into exploring the darker side of such matters. Ouija boards and late night escapades into cemeteries seemed the logical way to commence such a voyage. With little expectation of finding answers I began searching for anything that could tangibly substantiate the inner belief I already had in the reality of the spirit realm. It did not take long for whatever was on the other side of such a quest to answer the door as I began to knock. Radical, supernatural, and incredibly frightening occurrences began to transpire each and every time. Events portrayed in movies pertaining to the occult were becoming a normal part of my life. I realized I had opened a door into my life that had become a passage from that realm into mine. In an attempt to make the occurrences stop I quickly ceased my quest for answers and disengaged in all activities that had brought about this bridge between realms. Little did I know that once that door is opened, we do not possess the power, in and of ourselves, to close it.

In the following years my spiritual life was limited to movies and books. Then, all of a sudden, a deep driving desire to write a book of my own seemed to spring forth from a seed planted within my soul. Without wasting any time I began typing words upon a screen, and page after page, followed by chapter after chapter, was formed. The story was that of a sociopath who had spent his life preying on women in the Chicago suburbs; only to one day become the unsuspecting prey of another sociopath, who was far more evil than he was. The book offered water from a deep and dark spiritual well. It allowed the reader to navigate a mind darker than the absence of light. As I was writing this manuscript I allowed some of my friends and patients a first look at the contents to give me feedback. One of these patients had relayed my storyline to an agent they knew, and shortly thereafter I was in this agent's office signing a three book contract.

The title of the book was The Darker Mind, a perfectly fitting name. This book had become the number one obsession of my life. Countless hours and nights were spent trying to capture the perfect words and sentences to create a mental pictorial in the minds of my readers.

After four arduous years the book had made its way into a hard, and soft cover manuscript strategically positioned on the most prominent shelves of the local bookstores. A book signing tour was also underway. A major event was scheduled for October 30, 2005 at the Superstore Barnes and Noble near my home. The date was strategic: Devil's night. The night before

Halloween provided a perfect launching theme. Massive advertising was displayed and paraded around town for the upcoming event. Billboards were splashed with the name and cover of the book; a pair of red eyes peering out from a black and ominous background had caught the attention of many. It was mere days before this book-signing event that my life would be turned upside down.

Chapter 2: But They Told Me Hell Wasn't Real!!!

October 26th 2005: a day I will never forget. The day the answers I was willing to pay almost anything to find would be simply given to me. The night before had been quite uneventful, at least to natural eyes. I had gone to sleep at about midnight. Suddenly, I found myself in a state that seemed more real than any naturally occurring event I had ever participated in. My physical body was lying fast asleep on the bed, but another part of me was awake, and about to be taken on an epic journey. In what some would call a dream, and others would call a vision, I found myself falling in what could only be described as a dark well cut into the deepest parts of the earth. The well was full of darkness, and was colder than anything I had ever experienced. The darkness was so absolute it seemed to have a tangible presence that could be touched.

I remember clearly to this day the thoughts that ravaged my mind as I continued to fall down this deep well. I recall thinking that I would not hit the bottom and die, because I already knew I was in a dream, and my belief back then was that no one could die in a dream; otherwise they would also die in real life. This was an old myth I had heard that seemed at the time to make sense. My senses would quickly be gathered to absolute attention, as the impossible came to be. My eyes caught sight of the bottom of the well for only a fraction of an instant as my body braced itself for a violent impact.

Mere moments later, I found myself face down impacted into the dirt and stone that had broken the fall. I remember fear capturing not only my mind, but every aspect of my being. I could feel the pain of the impact. My bones had shattered, and I quickly realized that I was paralyzed as a result. So many thoughts exploded within my mind. Countless scenarios of what I was experiencing were processed faster than the newest computer chip ever could. It was then that a combination of my senses ignited. Both sounds and smells began to demand a hold on my mind. One particularly disturbing sound began to erupt, and it became louder each second. The sound was like something dragging itself, approaching me from my right; it was accompanied by an intensifying putrid odor from the same direction. The gift of sight was to no avail as I tried desperately to ascertain the source: my neck was turned to the left, and my muscles were unresponsive.

Then a different sound erupted. I knew it to be a spoken language, but muffled and distorted, and definitely not one I had ever heard before. The fear I was already saturated in only intensified. A state of utter hopelessness engulfed me faster than an unforeseen avalanche overtakes a small town at the base of the largest mountain. I wanted desperately to cry for help, but my lips were frozen by panic. It was then that the sounds around me let me be utterly aware of the close proximity of the undisclosed entity. I could hear this hulking creature standing over me. As it was mere feet from me my eyes were able to catch a glimpse of this thing. I could see the outline of what appeared to be a large hand with incredibly horrifying claws coming towards my head. I knew that whatever was there was about to grab me, and I could only imagine the outcome to follow. A state of despair that I did not know was possible seemed to penetrate every pore of my skin. As I closed my eyes, resigning to an apparent horrid fate...it all stopped.

My body sprung up to seated position, sweat dripped down from my forehead; my body was again responding. My eyes roamed in an attempt to bring some sort of clarity to this event. The realization that I was again in my bed, and not in that God-forsaken well, brought such a state of immediate relief. My mind released an emotional anchor as my thoughts needed time to regroup. While I was relieved by the fact I was no longer experiencing the horror of being at the mercy of some abomination, the fear from the event again manifested itself within me. Somehow I knew that what I had just experienced was not just a dream. I felt as if I had been cast into a giant ominous blender with paranoia, fear, despair, and hopelessness.

Inside me I knew vividly that the experience was not mere coincidence, it demanded a pause from deep within me. It was there that a soft voice speaking to me, as if it were my very thoughts, relayed to me a message that I could not ignore: I was about to die that very day! There was no uncertainty dwelling in me at that moment. I knew what I had just heard in my inner thoughts was the absolute truth. The irony of the moment is that I did not spend a single minute trying to decipher who the messenger was, for the message itself was more than I could bear.

My eyes slowly gazed around the room, almost as if caught in a moment of complete mental disassociation, and it was there that my heart was captured. My gaze had come to rest upon the small silhouette of my 4-year-old daughter. I explicitly remember back then my feelings overpowered me, as I contemplated leaving my little girl alone in this cruel world. Abandonment was something I never wanted her to experience, for as a child my biological father had abandoned me, at the age of one. The wounds I had carried my whole life were a constant driving force to make sure I never passed such things on to my children. Yet here I was, staring at the most precious thing my natural eyes had ever seen, as she lay peacefully asleep, knowing that mere hours were separating me from being permanently ripped away from her. In a desperate and yet tender response I gathered her into my arms and held her as close to myself as I could without waking her. It was as if I wanted all the love of a lifetime to be passed on to my daughter by that very embrace. Tears began to flood my eyes and my cheeks became river beds to a stream of emotional pain and regret. I loved my children as much as I had ever dared to love. This moment permeated the silence of that cold October night. The other thing I vividly remembered was that I had gazed at the alarm clock as I came out of the vision, and noticed that it was exactly 3:00 am. This almost silent embrace only interrupted by muffled the sounds of a heartbroken man giving way to his deepest fears went on for close to five hours.

It was at approximately 8 am that my (then) wife woke up to see me holding my child as if I were overcome by an emotional catastrophe. With concern that was more for the child than for me, she inquired what was happening. My response was short and to the point: "I am about to die!" Words that would usually induce a response of mercy and concern, began instead to paint a look of annoyance on the face of the woman I had spent the last five years of my life with. The marriage had been dead for some time now, as adultery and distrust from both parties had severed whatever little hope had laced this relationship together. Compassion was something I no longer had come to expect from this woman I shared a house with. My desire to converse with her at that moment was little at best. My heart instead was pouring whatever love it had into my child. The sound of my wife's voice relayed verbally the annoyance her facial gestures had already revealed. Her words brought little comfort: "Go to the doctor". I reported to her that I WAS a doctor and that I was not physically sick. After an attempt to relay the circumstances of the last five hours, I realized that it was fruitless. I then just told her to forget anything I had said, and to ignore me and let me be. During this verbal exchange the sounds of our voices had reached out and summoned my daughter back to a state of consciousness. Her precious eyes opened mere inches from mine. Tears again erupted from tear glands that had never worked so hard. A loving silent stare reflected in my daughter's eyes. Her little mouth began to allow a smile to form in response. It was in that moment that

Craig Stasio

I would have given anything to not be forced into separating from my little one.

My daughter had a preschool Halloween party scheduled that morning; I was going to attend with her. Trying with everything I could to hold back my deepest emotional fears, I helped get her ready for preschool and left to take her to the event. I remember hoping desperately that everything was only a hyper emotional event conjured up in my own thoughts, but deep within me I knew that not to be the case. As we entered the room designated for the party, children and parents seemed to blend into a collage of people large and small. I needed time to regroup emotionally, so with a tender kiss I released my daughter to play with her friends. A small table with miniature chairs, next to the table covered with concessions, was where my tired and worn body decided to rest. The uncomfortability of the small chair was dismal compared to the emotional torment ripping me apart at the seams. I watched my child play with her friends, as every so often she looked back to check on her daddy to make sure he was okay. The dialogue at the table between the other parents was something that my consuming emotions couldn't possibly allow me a glimmer of interest in. I ransacked my own memories and thoughts trying to find a solution to the apparent unavoidable fate that had come to call upon me, but to no avail.

This would go on till about 10:15 am when my tumult of thoughts was broken by the ringing of my cell phone. The number calling was my main chiropractic office. I was not scheduled to work until 3 pm that day, and I had set the time aside for my daughter. Reluctantly I answered the call. My manager seemed quite perplexed and distraught on the other end of the line as she explained the situation to me. She proceeded to tell me that a woman I did not know had called the office mere minutes prior. The woman had expressed that she needed to talk to me in the most urgent of ways. When my manager had told her that I would not be in till 3 pm she became severely agitated. She told my manager in a very authoritative tone that she could not wait till 3 pm, and that it was more urgent than she could ever understand that she talk to me. My manager tried to gather a message to relay to me, but the woman was unwilling to give it to anyone but me. Trying to give credibility to her urgency, the woman revealed to my manager that she had met her once years ago at a coffee shop, where she had a small booth set up as a psychic. This must have been the determining factor that allowed her to pierce the shielding my manager would have done normally during one of my mornings off. My state of panic that morning allowed for no other concerns to captivate my emotions, even as strange as this seemingly random phone call was. Little did I know how tied in to the previous night's events this phone call actually was. I initially tried to brush my manager off and to tell her to get rid of the lady herself, but her insistence on me talking to this stranger was delivered with a stringent resolve. Reluctantly, I agreed to call this unknown woman.

As I dialed the phone number I never expected what was to follow. An older sounding woman answered, and introduced herself by name. My initial response was one of annoyance, as I was accustomed to so many telemarketers and solicitors masking themselves as other people to force me into a conversation. I asked her what she wanted. Her response was that it was urgent that I come and meet with her in person as soon as possible, but she would not tell me why. This conversation would have normally cast me into confusion and fear, but on that morning my life had already been swept up in an untamable whirlwind of emotions and events. After multiple attempts to get me to come to her residence to receive the urgent message my response always stayed the same: that I was not interested. It was then, as a last resort, the woman spoke words that I can never forget.

"I will never forgive myself if I do not tell you, you are about to die!"

Chapter 3: The Day I Died

My attention was now all hers. Maybe this was an answer as to how to escape the fate before me. The wonder of how this stranger I had never met knew what was going on with me never crossed my mind; that she might have a way to help me avoid death was all I cared about. I began to ask her what I could do to stop it. Her response was that she did not know if it could be stopped, but that I should come by and talk to her immediately. She also said that she saw me dying at 1 pm. A quick glance at my watch...it was now 10:45 am. After a quick decision making exchange within my own thoughts, I declined the offer. A little more than two hours remained in the hourglass of my life. I wanted to spend that time alone with my children. I informed the woman that if she found any way to help me to go to my office and my manager would direct her to my home. I then thanked her for the message and hung up the call. Without delay I plucked my daughter from the miniature party and headed home.

To take you through the thoughts in my mind on the car ride home would take up its own book. Let it suffice you to know, that I felt lost in a place where I had lost all control in each and every way possible. The fifteen-minute car ride home was externally as silent as a cricket-less night in a deserted country plain, but inside, thoughts and emotions rallied vigorously to be heard in the forum of my mind. Not even Julius Caesar had ever had a more tumultuous gathering of voices.

I remember turning my key in the lock to open the door to my home. As I entered the foyer, I froze in my steps for a minute--I had finally surrendered to my fate; I knew there was no way out of my horrid predicament. It was in that very moment that I found an inner pause. The following moments would forever change the path of my life. Everything I thought to be empirical truth was now cast into a pool of doubt. Without really understanding how it happened to this very day, I found myself lying face down on the carpet of my den. I remember the texture of the rugged grain carpet against my face. I remember feeling the little ankles of my daughter gripped by both of my clenched hands as she stood over her daddy and watched in silence. An event was unfolding on that floor that I myself did not understand. An unseen force seemed to have intervened, I felt like I was almost being puppeteered by a powerful invisible presence. I could discern that whatever was there was so very powerful, even more overpowering than the fear that had seized me for the past 8 hours. I remember feeling my body overcome by this presence as I began to shake uncontrollably. Tears like never before sprang forth.

It was then that my shaking lips were called to speak. Words that I will never forget were expelled in that instant. Things were spoken that my mind did not understand. A power compelled me to speak such things, a combination of fear and remorse parted my lips to allow the words exit. I still remember hearing these unforgettable words. "Jesus, I am sorry!" was the first sentence to form from within and make its way out to become spoken sound. I could hear the words in my mind, but it was almost as if they were being spoken from someone else in control of my mouth. Then, as before, more words erupted:

"God I am so sorry that Jesus had to be crucified because of me!"

"I know I deserve to go to Hell, and if you still have to send me, still know that I am sorry!" It was in that intense moment that my wife entered the den captivated by the sounds radiating throughout the home.

In a state of anger she began to scream at me to stop! Truthfully, in that moment I was so overcome by things that I did not understand, that normal processing of my thoughts was unavailable to me. I could hear my wife continuing to scream for me to stop whatever I was doing, and to get up off the floor. I also remember my daughter still caught in a silent gaze, looking down on her dad. I remember desperately trying to understand what was happening.

It was then that a loud knocking of the door grabbed our attention. While wiping away countless tears with the sleeve of my shirt, and simultaneously rising from the floor, I made my way to answer the door, more confused than I had ever been in my life. As the knob turned and the hinges began to separate, there stood my manager, with a very large and imposing looking woman right behind her.

My manager quickly introduced her to me as being the woman on the phone. I invited them in without really understanding why. My mind was still caught up processing the experience on the den floor. The words that I had spoken seemed to replay themselves in my thoughts without end. I did not know in that instant if it was a wise idea to welcome that stranger into my home, but a desperation that was greater than reason seemed to direct my actions. I did not know what was happening, nor if anything had changed from moments before. Was death still coming to claim me? Had this stranger brought a ray of hope? What was the meaning of the event moments ago in the den? These were but some of the countless questions swirling in a frenzied storm within my mind. I did not know how to proceed, but I figured that the stranger here might be able to offer some insight, as she was the only other person there that actually had some understanding or belief in what was happening to me that morning.

With a semi state of silence assisted by facial and body gestures, I directed her to follow me into the basement of my home. Simultaneously, I directed my wife and manager to stay upstairs with the children. I knew that they did not understand or believe what was happening, and I did not have the time to explain it to them. I knew that if things were still headed down the same path that I had only one hour of life left. As I closed the door to the basement I made my way down the carpeted stairs and towards the poker table. I invited the woman to sit across from me. A state of awkwardness filled the room, but other feelings far more compelling drowned it out.

I began to ask her why I was going to die. I also asked again if she had found a way to help. Not for an instant did it dawn on me to tell her what had just happened in the den upstairs. She began to speak to me of things, most of which I do not even remember. Not five minutes after our conversation had begun, did the psychic begin to act agitated and bizarre. You would think that nothing any stranger could happen on a day like that, but that was not to be the case. She began to tremble and closed her eyes. Her voice also began to change, to a lower pitch, replacing the higher one there mere seconds ago.

"If you change your ways this can all be changed."

These were the words she would speak in a voice I knew not to be hers. She appeared to be coming in and out of a trance and began to tell me that these words were coming to me from a fatherly presence. I immediately processed the possible options of who that could be. My biological dad and step dad were both still alive, ruling them out. The next people to cross my mind were my grandfathers. They had both passed away, but I knew neither of them to be religious in any way. That was about as far as my mental exploration would allow itself to dig for answers.

It was then that things became really crazy. The door to the basement flung open abruptly, as my wife made her way downstairs in a frantic pace, her face filled with panic. All the alarms in the house had begun screeching with the digital readout showing it was 1 pm.

Yet it was not 1 pm yet.

And nobody had set them.

I admonished her to go back upstairs, as I tried not to explode in the panic overtaking me. As the door closed, again I quickly made my way back to the table. Again I sat down directly in front of this strange woman. It was exactly then that the inexplicable multiplied a hundredfold and invaded my physical body.

I remember looking into the face of the woman, as what appeared to be an incredibly powerful light began to shine behind me. I remember the face of the psychic as she looked over my shoulder, frozen in awe. I would have turned around to see what was behind me, but I myself was locked still in my chair. Not only could I discern the brightness of whatever was behind me, but now I could feel its merging with me. I will do the best I can to explain the following moments, but know that no words could ever explain this event in its fullness.

As this presence merged with me I entered a state very similar to when I was falling in the dark well the night before. I knew I was no longer seated at the poker table in my basement. I was suspended in what appeared to be thin air. I was surrounded by the purest and clearest light I had ever seen. I could look in every direction farther than I ever could with my natural eyes, and all I could see was bright, golden colored light. You would think I would have been encased again in fear like the night before, but this time was different. A tremendous sense of peace enveloped me from head to toe. Joy and love like I had never felt before flooded my being. I know in that moment I did not speak, although my thoughts were not so silent. I recalled asking a question deep within my own mind: "Where am I?" I did not expect a response to this internal question. Instantly the sound of my own thoughts answered: "You are in Me."

The encasing shell of peace surrounding me kept me from any sense of panic. I felt like a little child asking questions to an authoritative adult in the safest of settings. Again my thoughts would propel a question, but this time an expectation of bilateral mental dialogue was expected: "Who are you?" Again instantly the answer transpired: "I am God." Such a simple answer... yet so complex, I did not know how to proceed with another question. The voice then relayed to me that He was going to send me back. I immediately pleaded with Him not to! I begged Him to please let me stay there with Him. But He told me that He had work for me to do with Him, things that were important to Him.

In a resigning and conceding fashion I agreed to His will, and all of a sudden I felt myself being reinserted into my carnal body. Simultaneously I could feel that the bright light, previously behind me, had permeated me entirely, and what I can only describe as Velcro covered claws being ripped out of me from my chest and belly. This light moved through me as through a sponge, releasing these claws that had desperately tried to hold on to me. Suddenly I felt so indescribably free. Next came an intense and overpowering feeling of something like an invisible cascade of water fall upon me, and as it did I felt a washing in the innermost part of my being. I literally felt like I had just lost 100 pounds. The time between events to process one from the next never happened. Like falling dominoes these steps happened in rapid, unrelenting fashion.

It was then that crazy got even crazier. A ring of visible light surrounded me in that dim basement about 20 feet in diameter. The psychic who till this moment had been locked down in a silent stupor spoke out with vigor: "Can you see what's happening?!"

My response was immediate: "I can see the ring of light all around me!"

The woman shouted out: "You are surrounded by angels."

I truly do not know how I responded to that statement emotionally, except that I was overcome and swept away in the moment, with no understanding as to what was happening. The woman then began to speak again, but this time I had no desire or intention to listen. Quickly, I made my way upstairs to find that my wife had now called her mother and sister over while I was in the basement. The members of this newly formed crowd had each taken a seat at my kitchen table, directly in front of the opening to the basement door. Each of them directed a silent, concerned stare in my direction. I responded with a stare of utter awe and confusion back at them, also bridled in absolute silence.

My wife then was the first to act. Cautiously she got out of her chair and made her way towards me. As she approached me I could see the look of absolute panic in her eyes. She positioned herself right in front of me, and staring right into my eyes she spoke: "Where is my husband? Is he dead? Who ARE you?"

I could hear the questions being asked to me. The fact that she did not recognize me would usually cause a person to be distraught, but in that moment so many things were running through my thoughts I simply responded emphatically, "Honey it's me!" Again, she began to repeat the questions, this time reaching forward and grabbing at my shoulders, violently shaking me. My answer was the same. Even more frantically she continued to barrage me with the same questions, but as she continued, I had turned my gaze towards the kitchen table.

I was astounded by what was to follow: My eyes came to rest upon my mother-in-law, a woman that over recent years had become nothing less than an archenemy to me. In that moment everything around me seemed to stop. I was overcome by a brotherly love for that woman, a love I had never felt for anyone before. Something so seemingly small when compared to the rest of the day's events was the one thing that left me in a state of awe. I could not understand how this was possible, while knowing that it was absolutely happening.

Another amazing revelation suddenly hit my heart; I knew that I no longer had any sin. These words were not spoken to me, but this was a truth that I knew was absolute in that moment. My agitated wife kept on with insistent demands for answers to the questions I could not answer. I walked away from the small bevy of people, and towards the bedroom. My bed seemed the best place to settle my ever so shaken self. Internal reflection and self-exploration began to take place. My mind seemed to be caught in the state of a computer that had malfunctioned trying to reboot. I had no idea as to what had happened to me, however, I was still alive and it was now past 1 pm. Close to three hours passed by, as I laid in silence alone in my bedroom, while outside in the kitchen the fervent dialogue about me continued. At about four in the afternoon, the visitors would finally leave my home, at which point my wife again began to offer insistent demands for answers that I could not give her.

Peacefully I got up from the bed and made my way again into the den, where mere hours ago I had found myself sprawled out on the floor. I had never felt so confused and helpless in all my life like that day. There in front of me was the manuscript I had written. My major event was but 4 days away, a book signing at Barnes and Noble. I wanted to forget the whole crazy day, as I did not understand anything that had happened. In the days to follow, in an attempt to return to my normal life, I started to plan more speaking engagements to promote my book. The rest of that evening would come to pass and eventually I would go to sleep, hoping not to have another episode with the dark well.

Chapter 4: The Book Signing with a Demon

That night passed uneventfully. The morning would come as it had so many times before. My children would awaken and softly push and pull at their dad until he would wake up and spend time with them. My first waking thought was of escaping death, and yet another sunrise was granted for me to see and enjoy. A thorough recap of the prior day's event was then immediately underway. I pondered if the events had actually taken place? The state and behavior of my wife quickly confirmed everything I remembered.

Upon arriving at my office I would close the door to my office and sit at my desk in silence with nothing more than my Tim Horton's cup of coffee. I had no idea what to do with what had just happened to me. Where could I even go to figure it out, and who possibly could I talk to about it in hope to find answers? My manager made whatever small attempt she could muster to try and encourage me, while she herself started to question if I had gone insane. Many hours of that day were spent alone in the dark of a secluded office pondering and processing so many things. 7 pm would eventually come and the 25-minute ride home from work would commence in a car that would usually be filled with sounds from the radio that this night would be filled with silence. The following two days would look extremely similar to that day with no other crazy events, but then came the day of the major book signing and the beginning of understanding what was now happening to my life.

The morning of October 30th began early, with nervousness allowing little sleep the night before. The day of the anticipated book venture was here. A signing table, and cases of books were put into the back of my car, and off I went to the Barnes and Noble not more than 10 minutes from my home. The manager allowed me an early entrance into the location to set up my signing and promotion area. With anticipation I eagerly awaited for 10 am to allow the doors to open. In the back of my mind the events from 4 day's prior still lingered, but the signing now overcame anything else going on in my mind. For close to ten hours the signing unfolded with countless readers gathering to purchase the book, and get it signed. The event was a great success. The manager of the store approached me at about 6 pm and relayed to me that it had been the biggest turnout that store had ever witnessed. The manager also offered for me to come back whenever I wanted to have another signing.

The store was scheduled to close at 10 pm, a little more than two hours away, when fate again decided to invade my life in the most incredible of ways. A medium sized crowd of about 30 people including friends and family were gathered around my table. I was signing a copy of the book with my back positioned towards the front door to the store. Without seeing anything with my natural eyes a severe and immediate chill ran down my spine. Without understanding how I knew what was happening, I was completely and absolutely aware of one thing with all my being: the creature in the vision with the dark well had walked into that book store.

My hand stopped. The books just purchased by eager fans and awaiting my autograph set before me in piles sat dumb. My body in a rapid jerking fashion turned in the direction of the front door to the store. A man in his late twenties had just entered the store. Nothing about him seemed strange to the natural eye at first. His clothes were casual; a flannel shirt and rugged jeans. My eyes fixed upon him with absolute attentiveness. Sensing the presence of that being in the store only intensified as he slowly walked towards me. As he got within 15 feet of my signing table he stopped and directed his face at the floor. No one had noticed him yet, that is, except me.

People around me kept on with whatever they were doing as if nothing were happening. My attention was undivided from the stranger. Every question and request directed at me were ignored and purged before my mind could even give them cadence. It was then that the stranger began to show his true colors.

With a tone of voice that started out soft and muffled he began to speak as if caught in a chant. His eyes continued to gaze at the floor as his voice became more and more loud and clear. The chant was regarding topics of mysticism and witchcraft. The people around him and that stood between him and my signing table began to part like the Red Sea. People knew that something was wrong with him but they had no idea as to what it was.

The feeling of fear that had so captivated me when I was caught in that well was again gripping me to my very core. Why was it there? Was it inside this man? Or was it the man himself? So many questions flooded my mind. What was I to do? How had it found me? Was death again set on taking me?

The chant became loud enough that everyone could no longer ignore or discard it within the bounds of social etiquette. Fear directed me to dart and hide behind members of the parting crowd before this man would lift his gaze and catch sight of me. Blanketed in fear as I was, I still managed to launch a question from behind the table.

"Where did you read about these things?"

The question seemed to give him pause. He stopped the ritualistic self-dialogue and raised his gaze towards the ceiling. His eyes that had been closed now slowly opened as he began to speak again. I recall the words he spoke as they pierced the store's silence; all eyes were now on him. The manager was trying to decide what to do as I could see a deep concern upon his face, but he was unable to decide on a course of action and so did nothing. The strange man now raised his voice even louder than before as he began to answer my question.

"Read? I need not read, for my power comes from a higher source. I draw from the stars and the constellations of the heavens, for I am the fallen left arm of Jehovah."

As he finished that statement, he proceeded to walk in my direction and directed his piercing gaze at me. Those five to six steps seemed to take forever as he finally stopped not more than 3 feet directly in front of me. I wanted to run with every fiber of my being, but something kept me pinned to that floor mere feet from fear incarnate. His mouth again began to move as he raised his right hand and pointed his index finger no more than 3 inches from my nose.

"And now you know exactly who I am."

Chapter 5: Learning to Pray and using my "Spider Sense"

I abruptly found my manager who was there to oversee the event, and within minutes I was shouting to her, "Shut it down! Shut it down! NOW!" Trying to not show the fear that had overtaken me, I hurried to my car and drove straight home. Afterward, I laid silent in bed, while my wife slept, and my little daughter laid between us. I can't even begin to express my emotional state. All of my life my intellectual gifting had always allowed me to navigate situations where others could not. That night, the incredible mind I had was of no value to me. I felt like a child lost and alone in the woods in the dead of night. For five long hours I basked in this state of confusion and fear, until finally at 2:05 am the first ray of hope interjected in the dark hopelessness of the night. The one thing that should have made sense days ago now was so evident. In a rare act of humility I began to pray. I don't know if I had ever prayed as an adult before that night.

It was here that the reality of my new life would forever be forged. My hands would clasp themselves as if to acknowledge I was now crying out for help to someone far greater than me, and that they deserved reverence. That first prayer was one I will never forget.

"God, why are demons after me? I am sure that it has something to do with You, but that's okay. Could You please keep me safe, and if there are any of them coming after my children could You please get them away from them?"

As I closed this simple prayer I knew that there was a required stamp to make sure it got to where I had sent it. I knew that without this stamp the prayer would not produce any response, so without hesitation the verbal stamp was spoken: "In Jesus' Name."

Little did I know how fast a response can come when faith accompanies the placing of that verbal stamp on a prayer. Before I could unclench my hands, as I opened my eyes, the reality of my God manifested itself. My four year old daughter was sleeping no more than a foot from me with her back facing me. The prayer I had just spoken was in a tone resembling a soft whisper, allowing no one other than me and God to hear it. My daughter's body began to move, but in a way that is anatomically not possible. My background in physics, science, and anatomy only helped me to understand that what I was observing was supernatural. As if a giant invisible spatula had inserted itself under my little girl I witnessed her entire body flip 180 degrees in one fluid motion without a single muscle contracting. The past week had shown me that my perception of reality was drastically wrong, and that the impossible and bizarre could actually become the normal in one's life. As I observed this unnatural movement of my child my mind and heart braced itself for whatever was to come next.

The possibilities were endless as to what I would be cast into next, but I had resigned myself to stand in faith, and fight whatever it was. My eyes fixed themselves on my daughter's face as she continued to lay there fast asleep, though now she was facing me. Her little mouth then opened and without her awakening a screeching sound like a huge bird reverberated through the bedroom. I quickly grabbed my ears in fear that the sound was so loud it would damage my tympanic membranes, as well as shatter every window and glass door in the house. The screeching scream would last not more than 7 to 8 seconds and then what appeared to be dark mist or fog came out of her and I was thrown from my bed, slammed into a dresser, and landed on the floor. My eyes followed the dark mist as it moved towards the bedroom window, and eventually passed through it. The window was closed yet the heavy blinds shook as the fog passed through them.

Fear again exploded upon me, but this time it was not strong enough to paralyze me. The love and concern for my child overtook all other emotions. By now my wife had awoken as well, and was screaming irrationally. Quickly, I catapulted myself back upon the bed, and grabbed my little girl in a protective response. I then was able to make out my wife's screams:

"What is happening?!"

I asked her if she had heard the screeching sound, but she said she witnessed me getting thrown off the bed by something she could not see.

The next few hours were spent trying desperately to understand what had just happened, and even more importantly, what was to come? A piece of the puzzle that made me ponder more than the others was why was I the only one to see and hear the full event? Eventually, the night would again become a time that would allow sleep. Following only a few hours of intermittent consciousness I made a decision: I was going to find out as much as I could about this God that I had prayed to.

My arrival at the main chiropractic office was earlier than usual. I was in a state of aware vigilance that even my normal cup of morning coffee could not supplement. Countless questions swirled inside my head, with even more waiting their turn. Everyone I had talked to thought I was crazy and was quickly becoming annoyed with me, so there was only one way to get to the bottom of all this: the Bible. The most sold and known book in the entire world was also the most ignored. Almost everyone had one somewhere packed away with dust. I remembered I had received one at premarital counseling in the Lutheran church before my second marriage. That book had been retrieved before I left my home that morning. The smallest irony was that as I opened the cover there was my name inscribed on the inside. Not once since receiving it had I dared to read it. My entire Christian experience up to this time was attending a few makeshift home gatherings of self-professed Christians as a child until the age of 6. My knowledge of Christianity was mostly through movies like The Ten Commandments and Jesus of Nazareth, the only other source of any information whether true or false was through the movies about end days and demonic possession. The time had now come to stop avoiding; time to actually dare to allow my own eyes to read the words in that controversial manuscript.

So many pages to choose where to start from... so many chapters. Common sense would tell me to start in the beginning and read through it as I had countless books before; for some reason I just knew that was not the best way.

The wildest thing had begun to happen the moment I was surrounded by the circle of visible light in the basement days ago. The best way to describe it would be by using a memory from my childhood. As a kid I was a comic book fanatic, especially when it came to Spider-Man. I would read multiple volumes in bed at night and go to sleep wondering how cool it would be to have super powers like his. One of these was what he called a "Spider-Sense." This supernatural ability would warn him when danger was coming that he could not see or hear. His head would start to tingle as a sign to alert him. A similar ability had been imparted to me as of result of the recent events. My head would have an intense buzzing-like sensation right before something bizarre would happen to me. This "buzzing" had been very strong right before my daughter's body flipped in bed and the black mist came out of her. At first when this sensation occurred I was concerned I was having a mild stroke. Over time the sensations would continue to come and go with no pain or any other neurological signs or symptoms so I knew it not to be a stroke. I was mystified.

As I grabbed the Bible and sat down at my desk preparing to open it, something similar to that tingling began. It was like I had a Morse code channel with the spirit realm where the signal being sent was one only I could pick up on. It was so wild. But then again, what hadn't been in the last week? I was starting to learn to stop fighting these things, and instead try to understand them. That invisible coded message seemed to be leading me to read the last book of the Bible first. That made no sense to me in the natural. Why ruin the whole book by reading how it ends? That was something I never did, and it irked me when people would tell me a book's ending and ruin it for me. This time, though, was different. And that crazy supernatural sense I now had, was clearly directing me to the Book of Revelation.

Chapter 6 :The Book of Revelation

My eyes began a physical exploration of the typed words transposed onto the waxy pages. The sentences and paragraphs flowed together in the most incredible of ways. I quickly was caught up in the most exhilarating story I had ever read. The story painted majestic pictures within my mind. As I continued to read, I realized that without any doubt what I was reading was not a compilation of bedtime stories and fiction. It was empirical truth. I did not know how it was that I knew this, except that I knew it with every fiber of my being.

I remained caught in a state of utter awe as I read the words Jesus relayed to His Apostle John. The vision John had, as he stood before this Jesus that had been resurrected and taken up to Heaven left me speechless. This man that claimed to be the Son of God was powerful. As I continued to read the pages, I knew beyond any doubt, that He was exactly who He claimed to be. I was caught away, emotionally lost in the splendor of the King He was. I remembered the end of my prayer the night before: that I had supernaturally known to invoke His name. I was getting my first real look at the One I was praying to. I was so overtaken that I had to pause and evaluate. I felt as if I had reached a fork in the road of my very life.

Everything I thought I knew before to be true, now in light of what had been happening to me, seemed to all be at best, possible truths, and therefore, also possible deceptions. Was I willing to throw away 38 years of mental building blocks? Was I willing to erase it all like an Etch-A-Sketch screen and start over? My pride in being so knowledgeable was now challenged like never before. If this Jesus was real, then my whole life had been founded on lies and deceptions. I had been duped on a level I couldn't have previously even imagined.

The answer as to what to do did not take long to come to me; I had the most determined and insatiable desire to have raw and uncorrupted truth. In that moment I felt as if a cloak of humility had been gently laid upon my shoulders. I was willing to accept that everything in my life might have been based on lies and half-truths, because now I was staring face to face with the words on those pages, knowing that they were the absolute truth. I felt like a child that had just stumbled on to the greatest treasure I could ever imagine.

The rest of that wonderful late October morning was spent locked away in my personal office alone with that incredible book, scavenging through the pages like a desperate gold digger in the spirit realm. I dared to believe everything I was reading. Doubt and conjecture as to the truth of Scripture were quickly cast outside that office, and I chose to banish them from my new life. The Jesus in the Book of Revelation was someone that no amount of words alone could ever describe. That Jesus was the Son of the God. He had spoken to me when I was caught away in the bright golden light during the experience in my basement. That God had spoken to me, the worst of sinners, a man that had done nothing but use his 38 years on this earth to conduct one form of debauchery after another.

Why would the Father of Jesus want anything to do with me? A million reasons could be given as to why it was all too good to be true, but there was one that silenced them all: the fact that here I was still alive. And I wanted to read the Bible with an uncanny attentiveness. I had no idea where the new life I was discovering would lead me to; nonetheless I was so excited to find out. The Book of Revelation continued to unfold in my mind and heart as I read on. The awesome depictions of Heaven with the resurrected Jesus sitting on the throne next to His Father, the eternal, uncreated, God of all the Universe, left me speechless; all the angels worshipping Jesus, and giving Him glory, honor, and power claiming that He was worthy to receive such things. This was truly a king that deserved to be bowed to. For the first time in my life I had found someone that I knew was far more important than anything I could ever have strived to become. I had found the one person that I could yield to. I wanted to know His cause and to find out everything I could about Him. I wanted to have a chance to be on His team, regardless of where that would lead me, or the cost. I had finally found a purpose for my very existence, a cause that I could give myself completely to with reckless abandon. As the pages continued, the description of the things to come upon the Earth was breathtaking: judgment seals, trumpets, and bowls of wrath, all being released from Heaven upon the Earth, all at the command of this powerful Jesus. Thoughts that this tribulation could happen within my lifetime, that it wasn't a recounting of times past, or a symbolic allegory, shocked me. Without any doubt I knew He had every legal right to do this, no matter how horrifying it appeared. Who was I to question the actions of this King of Heaven? The One who sat in authority at the right hand of God Almighty? Attentively I read each judgment released upon what Jesus deemed an evil mankind. I knew that I was one of those people that He was punishing with an unrelenting rage, and yet, I knew that I actually wasn't one of them...anymore.

I continued to read that during that time there would be others that had not turned against Jesus, and that they would be protected from all these judgments issuing from Him. Those people would undergo a vivid persecution from the people that hated Jesus, and they would be led by the Antichrist. I was so glad to not be an enemy of Jesus any more. Death and persecution at the hands of evil people and the Antichrist seemed like nothing in comparison to the judgments I had somehow avoided. Never had any book, movie, or song completely engulfed me like The Book of Revelation in the Bible. Eventually the story would tell of the climax of all time. While calamity and destruction were at their peak of devastating all creation, an event that all mankind for all eternity would never forget would take place.

I read Chapter 19 slowly and in complete wonder. This Jesus would part the very skies above, shutting down the sun and moon from shining. The light radiating from Him alone would cause the entire planet to see Him in awesome glory. The description of His power and authority as He marched from Heaven itself left me speechless. This King was coming to wage war against His enemies and save His people. I wanted to be one of His people in that moment with everything in me. The thought of Jesus coming to rescue me and others like me from impending doom brought me to tears. For the first time in my life I felt truly safe. This Jesus was now watching over me from Heaven, and I was no longer His enemy. The closing chapters would tell of life after His return to earth, and another age where humanity would again undergo a temptation from the devil, only to have everyone who rebels against Jesus destroyed through fire raining down on them from Heaven. Finally, the end of the story, Chapters 21 and 22, depict the coming of a new Earth where Heaven itself comes down to join our planet. God the Father comes down to live with us, and Jesus is the King of this new earth forever, a land filled with peace, joy, and love. I remembered the feelings I had when I was caught up in that bright light. The emotions I felt were exactly those: peace, love, and joy in an indescribable magnitude. I had been given a sneak preview of what it was going to be like. I smiled with joy. That state of absolute bliss was awaiting me on the other side with Jesus as my awesome King. My life in that moment had taken on more meaning than I could have ever previously imagined.

Chapter 7: "Son, I love you."

Throughout the morning most of my staff kept knocking at the closed office door as I sat alone and read. Repeatedly they offered their concerns about me, referencing that I was secluding myself. Again and again I would smile and tell them to close the door. All I wanted to do is read The Book of Revelation again and again to discover the essence of this great Jesus. My mind and heart began to tremble at the thought of one day standing face to face with Him. Then I remembered that months prior I had stumbled on a song that had captivated me that spoke of exactly such a moment. The title of the song was "I Can Only Imagine" by MercyMe. The lyrics depicted a day when each member of humanity would stand before Jesus. The lyrics described potential outcomes of such an encounter: dancing, awe, falling in worship. I remember purchasing the CD, and sometimes listening to it for hours at a time. At the time I didn't understand why that song had such a pull on me, but it had been so powerful I could not avoid it. Little did I know it was but one of the many bread crumbs that God had lain before me to lead me home. As I pondered on that very fact, I realized there had been many of these so called bread crumbs, all strategically put in the path I was traveling. I then recalled another one.

A month or so prior I had abruptly woken up in the middle of the night. I was brought to a state of complete awareness from a deep sleep. I had no idea what had caused me to awaken, but my senses were forced into an immediate state of awareness. My rapid rising to a seated position had also awakened my wife. As I sat there in bed trying to figure out why I was awakened the strangest thing happened; my bedroom television turned itself on. I remember looking at the remote control laying innocently on the nightstand. My mind wondered what was going on, for I could feel something supernatural was taking place. The cable box then started changing channels on its own. My wife and I sat speechless, watching. The cable box would eventually come to stop on a channel in the 300 range. That stood out to me because I never watched those channels. The 300s were reserved for religious channels and music stations, neither of which interested me in the least. My eyes locked on the screen as a speaker appeared and shouted words that pierced my soul: "You need Jesus!" I had leapt out of bed to turn the television off. With shaking hands I unplugged both the television and the cable box. After a very brief discussion with my wife, she discarded the whole thing as coincidence. Long after she fell asleep, I laid there knowing it was not a mere random event. I could not get the words out of my mind. Every scientific possibility had been exhausted in my mind, none of which offered a solution. I guess I chose to just continue in my life and see what happened. Little did I know that Heaven was in the process of recruiting this sinner to come home, and to become part of something (and someone) greater than I could suppose.

I continued my days at the office, quickly treating patients without offering the casual conversation that I had become well known for, and that they were accustomed to. I had more important things waiting for me back in that silent office. There were so many other pages in that awesome book I hadn't read yet. I often read and re-read The Book of Revelation. This had become the one obsession in my entire life that was actually good. It provoked curiosity in me, how distraught my staff became at knowing I was reading the Bible. I had never seen all of them become more collectively agitated. Normally I would have sat down, and heard their concerns, engaging in a prolonged dialogue, in an attempt to lead them to see things my way. Now though, I really did not care what others thought of me, I just wanted to read that phenomenal book by myself. I would spend close to eight hours with my eyes and heart buried in that book, and upon my arrival at home I continued to do more of the same.

I realized that the passion for promoting my own book had become dimmed by the newfound one. A moment of reflection brought me to ponder how the great King in Heaven felt about the dark book I had written. Would He have approved if He were to crack the sky in that very moment? Where did this leave me? More importantly what was I to do with the book? Four years of countless hours were poured into that manuscript, not to mention the financial commitment. I had already invested close to $100,000 publishing, editing, marketing, and distributing it. My agent was in the process of sending it to major movie companies. Not to mention that I had already signed a three book contract with my agent. I had already started writing the other two.

I knew without any doubt that the book I had written was not something pleasing to that King seated in Majesty in Heaven. Did I really believe what I had read? How could I forget the judgments that were one day to come upon the earth? Surely the man that wrote that book would be one of them. Although I was the one to write that dark novel, I also knew that the man I was in that moment had not written it. I felt as if I had been granted a fresh new start at this crazy convoluted thing we call life. I decided in that moment I must concede this to the will of the great King. Now I had to find out exactly what that was.

I lay in bed awake and contemplative, choosing to seek the will of God for my life. Again I would undergo a radical transformation sparked by new revelation. My thoughts were on what my life would look like next, and what to do, as a subtle voice that sounded like my own thoughts begin to speak to me. Although I was mildly shocked, I still had a pretty good idea of who might be talking to me. I froze in silence, as even my own thoughts cleared the way for this other voice to speak unclouded. The first clear words to eloquently enter were: "Son, I love you." The very first word in this small sentence was one that carried such meaning I could not even possibly began to understand at that time. The "I love you" shook me to my very core. How was I supposed to respond? What was the spiritual and acceptable way to reply? Could I offer an: "I love you, too?" Could I really say that to the God of all the Universe since we had just met? Those words seemed to be a spiritual balm, something God decided to start applying to some of the deepest wounds inside my fragile and wounded heart. Those words would be so important to me for months and years later, but I didn't know it at the time. I allowed myself to crack a small smile, as the words again sprang forth from the silence in my mind. People had always tossed those words (I love you) around as freely and carelessly as a morning newspaper delivery boy on a bicycle. This time though I knew there was a meaning far deeper. I was being talked to by the Creator of the Universe! I was completely captured unlike anything before. I sat as silently as I could, hoping more words would follow.

I was afraid if I did or said anything the line would hang up. I was almost paralyzed in awe. As I lay anxiously and waited that soft mental voice would speak again: "Son, I love you." Again I found myself caught in an emotional labyrinth. How was I to respond? God had now spoken those words again. This time I felt compelled to reply: "God, I love you too". And then added: "Thank you for protecting me and my daughter from those demons." Surely that must have been what they were. What else could that black mist have been but an evil spirit? Most of that night was spent in short yet incredible exchanges of words, a mental discourse only mine to hear.

Chapter 8: Finding Other Believers and Being Under Cover

The next morning, even though only a few hours had been offered to replenish my now sleep deprived body you would have never been able to tell. I was alert and awakened, anxious to see the next crazy thing to happen to me. I entered my office that morning with a level of supernatural joy that permeated from my pores. I remember that morning very clearly. As I walked through the long lobby filled with chairs for patients that voice began to speak to me again. Sitting were two women in their late 20s (one of which had been a previous patient of mine). I am not sure why they were there that morning. Or should I more accurately say that I am not sure why they thought they were there? As I walked past them I froze in my steps, and turned around. For I split second I processed what I had just heard, and then like a little child my voice erupted in stupor:

"You two know God!"

A look of utter shock came over the two young women. They looked at me and asked me to repeat what I had just said.

"You two know God!" I replied again, this time a little louder than before, as excitement started to flood my being.

My next sentence was offered with the innocence of a child finding out Santa Clause is not real: "Why didn't you ever tell me you knew God?!"

A facial manifestation of immediate shock covered both of their faces, as they did not know how to respond.

Again my voice bellowed out:

"You two are like pastors or something, right?"

Their response now came from a puzzled face that also showed signs of the importance of the moment:

"How did you know that?"

"God told me!" I replied.

"Please come into my office and talk to me!" My invitation was that of an excited child.

I had finally found someone else that knew this God of the Bible; now maybe I could get some of my burning questions answered. A two to three hour exchange of words would fill the morning. The two women shared with me that they were Christian ministers in a small home church congregation. They seemed shocked at the boldness I demonstrated as I shared my story with them. They also told me that they had not held services in a while. Again the soft voice inside me spoke. The words would quickly make their way from my mind to my mouth:

"He told me to put myself under your wing."

And then: "What does that mean?" came blurting out of my mouth. After a final exchange of words they invited me to come over to their house at a later date to talk, and to see what this God of ours meant by that.

Finally I had found others like me! The forced solitude could now come to an end. I remember feeling almost betrayed that these two women had already known this God for some time and had never told me. My mind could not wrap itself around such a thing. But as they left my office I was encouraged at the prospect of future conversations. Being that it was Saturday, I returned home in the early afternoon. I sat in my house at the kitchen table with my Bible still opened to the great Book of Revelation. Shortly thereafter that soft voice made its way through my thoughts:

"Call Paul and tell him to come over."

Let me introduce you to Paul. He was my best friend now for almost twenty years. Any escapade I had embarked on during that period was almost always done with him. We shared everything, like brothers. He was a man of incredible emotional depth, which had always intrigued me. He was the one friend that allowed a relationship that would remain bilateral as we stepped out of shallow emotional waters into the deep ends of the pool of life. We both worked at the local seafood restaurant and attended community college together. One night we sat in a car after our shift ended and thoroughly discussed the possibility of God being real. That conversation went on well into the early morning hours as we simultaneously emptied twenty four cans of beer.

Over the years we had both become avid gamblers. Horse races and the craps tables at the local casino saw us more than our families. We would usually talk multiple times a day, but since the event in my basement we had not communicated at all. It was not until the voice in my head told me to call him did I realize our recent lack of communication. As I stepped to grab the phone I paused. I realized that it was Saturday afternoon. Every Saturday since I had known Paul he had spent his Saturdays from dawn till dusk with his Dad at a variety of horse racing tracks. It was almost like a gamblers holy day to him and his dad, nothing was ever allowed to interfere with their sacred day. It was time to really put this voice in my thoughts that I presumed to be God to the test. The voice was telling me to call Paul and invite him over.

Twenty years of history told me that there was no chance of him being home. Perplexed, confused, and with a small hint of doubt trying to creep in I turned the wheel over to faith and dialed the phone number.

It did not take long to find out if he was there, by the second ring the call was answered. With a smile on my face I began to speak, as the voice that had answered on the other end was his. Paul sounded surprised. His greeting was not a normal "Hello?", but instead he offered a: "How did you know I was home, dude?" It is hard to relay to you the improbability of this man not being at the race track on this day, even more improbable is the fact I had called him knowing he was. The mild confusion in his voice would soon increase as my voice joined the event.

"Paul, I need you to come over, there is something important I need to tell you."

His surprise quickly switched to concern:

"What's wrong? Are you okay?"

I did not want to disclose anything to him over the phone. I knew that the unction to call him by God had also specifically directed me to have him come over to my home first. The next few minutes were spent battling my friend as he tried to coerce me into doing the opposite, but my resolve won the battle of verbal tug of war. Reluctantly and annoyed Paul decided to yield, and told me he would be there in about an hour. As the phone was hung up, I knew I was about 60 minutes away from another one of those crazy experiences that had now invaded my life. Normally I would have obsessed about what was going to happen when Paul arrived, although I seem to be functioning quite differently than before now. A thriving desire to scavenge through the Bible for truth was still screaming out to be satisfied, so back to that incredible book I went. The hour would pass quickly, and the abrasive knock on the door that usually alerted me to Paul being on my porch echoed in the otherwise quiet house. As I unlocked the door with my hands, I began to emotionally prepare for whatever response my best friend would offer to what I was about to tell him.

Chapter 9: "Repent and be humble!"

As the doorway opened to the outside world, a brisk November breeze was the first thing to enter my home, depositing a few scattered leaves of various colors at my feet. My eyes then would come to rest upon the distraught face of another 38-year-old man. Paul knew something important was happening. I later found out that the whole hour was spent by him analyzing in his own thoughts the countless scenarios that could have led to that phone call one hour ago. Countless possibilities had presented themselves to him, all except the real one.

Paul persisted in requesting to know what was going on. I offered a half smile and silently directed him to the basement where we would have some privacy from my skeptical wife. I knew if this conversation had taken place upstairs in the living room she would have interjected repeatedly into our conversation. There I was again traveling down those 13 stairs that led to the basement where, a week ago, my life was put on a course where it would change forever. This conversation would not take place at the poker table though, the couch was the environ of choice. Our friendship had always been one that was built on trust, and transparency. Our discussion and debates were about as candid as two humans could have. This would sometimes turn into heated exchanges, nonetheless we both deeply valued the raw and open channel of communication we had developed over the years. I tried to offer a preparatory disclaimer to help set the stage for Paul to receive my story. Paul could feel the seriousness of the situation, so the serenity that I seemed to be radiating only confused him. After as much preparation as I could give him, I began to tell him everything that had taken place over the last week. At the end, Paul was left speechless, something that was as rare as the 29th of February. I could see his glossed over eyes as the mind behind them was racing. He knew I was serious about what I had just shared. Many times had we played pranks on each other, some of them incredibly elaborate ones, but he could absolutely tell that this was not one of them. I really did not know what else to do at this point. I sat and waited for a response from Paul as to what he thought of the whole thing.

As I sat there still and silent, my head began to tingle in a way that was impossible to ignore. It was quite a different sensation than before. It was not an uncomfortable sensation as when the demonized man walked into the bookstore. Instead, this time it felt soothing, while still very intense. Paul could see the look created by a combination of confusion, and intrigue, overtake my face. I lifted off the couch and to my feet, feeling as if my body was controlled by another. I must admit I was overcome by a barrage of sensations and emotions in that moment. Never had something like this taken place between us. Paul observed the whole process, and I could see a panic starting to grab hold of him. I did not know what to do, or what to say. I do recall what I did manage to muster up:

"Paul, I do not know what is going on!"

Then, before I could understand what was happening, a wild event unfolded once again. My mouth spouted words that did not come from my mind. There was no thought process that brought forth these next words leaving my mouth, but a force I could not resist overtook me and I yielded to it.

"Repent, and be humble before the Lord!"

What a wild sentence to come out of my mouth! My mind heard the words the same time Paul's ears did. What was going on? I was beside myself! The scenario was made even crazier by the fact that as I began to speak, my right index finger had extended itself in Paul's direction, as if to bring the silent exclamation point to the statement. I had never seen Paul so scared in my life. The supernatural was something that had always horrified him, he was about as vanilla as they come when dealing with anything from the unseen spiritual realm. This day though, he would not be able to run away and hide. It was going to be equally impossible for him to write off everything that was happening with me up to now as coincidence. I felt like I was a gigantic puppet. The fact someone else seemed to be controlling the motor function of my body was quite alarming, but a tremendous peace had overtaken me. I knew I was as safe as I could ever be. I again fixed my eyes on my friend and his panic was apparent. I tried to offer whatever help I could as I was able to speak:

"Paul, that was not me saying that! I don't know what is going on!"

He looked at me attentively. Normally he would interject in intense situations with a calculated humorous response, a coping mechanism. The seriousness of the moment would have absolutely brought about this type of response any other time, but not today. A tangible presence was there in the basement with us: an unseen power greater than any we had known. A sobering feeling overcame us both; we were left absolutely undone on the inside. Never had these two grown and independent men felt more like little vulnerable children! The word I would now use to describe the atmosphere in the basement that day was one, up to that point of my life, I knew nothing about: holy. Looking back now I know the word that would have described it would have been holy. The holy presence there was indescribable. As I write this part of the book I am in tears remembering the events. What a privilege to have had such an experience! The awesome nature of the event taking place right in front of my very eyes; that I was being allowed to be part of it, was something I could not grasp at the time, but that I would continually grow to understand.

As I stood there, half caught in some sort of trance, the inner stirring inside would began to swell again. Again, words would force their way out of my mouth for Paul to hear:

"Repent, and be humble before the Lord!"

The holy presence in the room became more evident than before. I had no idea what to do. I knew it was something that I could not stop--even though my body was involved in the delivery of this message--my mind was not. I knew what was happening was a potentially life changing event for both of us. I pondered who the Lord was that Paul was being ushered to, to humble himself before. I was not sure if it was God the Father, or His Son Jesus. Either way, I waited with an excited anticipation to see what would happen next. What was Paul thinking? More importantly, what was he going to do in lieu of what was being asked of him? It is so hard to relay to you the incredible intensity of the moment. Imagine your mouth speaking words to another person all on its own. The only reference I had ever had of such things was in movies where séance's were taking place, or where demon possessed people had the demon inside them speak through them. However, I knew that what was happening to me was neither of these situations. Someone very powerful was borrowing my body to conduct His business. I was a little scared, but the holy presence in the room accompanied by the supernatural peace gave me the ability to not crumple in fear. Paul finally began to speak:

"What should I do?"

Never had I seen Paul so humble. Never had he been so yielding to anyone or anything. The holy unseen presence in the room shook him to his core. I watched as tears began to form on this man's cheeks. He knew it was the very God we talked about so many years ago that was summoning him to this act of obedience. He also knew, in that moment, I was nothing more than a willing vessel, with the willing part being disputable in his mind.

Immediately as he had asked the question I heard the soft voice inside me began to speak to me:

"Tell him to humble himself like a little child."

I heard this directive so clearly, but I really did not understand what that meant, or how Paul could do what was being requested. Even though I had very little comprehension as to what I was about to say would elicit in response, I obeyed the small voice inside me, and told Paul what I was instructed. Paul looked at me with a silent glazed over look, as tears continued to form in his eyes. The voice inside me instructed me to tell him again, so I did. This second time I could see whatever veil was covering Paul's mind get ripped away. His response was immediate, as he fell to his knees to pray, and to surrender. His hand reached out to me, as he asked me if I would place my hands on his shoulders and pray with him. I had never done anything like this before; I was in uncharted waters of epic depth. It felt like I was trying to swim in the middle of a category five hurricane, but again the peace present there trumped all other emotions inside me. Almost like a knight being ordained by the king, I placed my hands on my best friend and prayed with him. He cried out to God for mercy as he felt a strong conviction about his sinful life. I could see the sorrow manifest itself on his face as he spoke in a muffled voice between the cascading tears. The event was precious and intimate, as I saw this grown man meet God as I had five days ago.

Paul would eventually rise back to his feet, and I was given one of the most gripping hugs I had ever received in my life, as he started to wipe the tears away from his face. I knew he was different than the man that had arrived at my front door, the same way I was a different man than the one that went down into my basement days ago. I could see a sparkle in his eyes, a glow of sorts, and not one brought on by the tears. I knew my best friend had actually had his own personal experience with God, Jesus. I was so happy and excited! My best friend now knew what had happened to me was real. I would not have to explain away my last five days trying to convince him of their authenticity. What would happen now? What are two 38-year-old men that just met God supposed to do? We were both perfectionists in our own mind, always wanting to be the absolute best at whatever we did. Whenever there was something we did together an unhealthy spirit of competition would always raise its ugly head. At the end of the prolonged embrace we sat in that basement and talked for hours, processing what had just taken place in our lives, and how to proceed from here. The final conclusion that we reached before Paul departed to head back home, was that we thought the next obvious step would be to find a church to attend. Paul took it upon himself to undertake the task of finding the right church for us. He left with another grateful hug, and told me he was going to make that his first priority in the morning, and that he would get back to me in the morning.

I could see my wife's look of distain as my friend left. Now there were two of us that she would call crazy. She had always thought we were over the top in anything we did, so why should this time be any different she thought. Again, as I had for the last five days, I tried to convince her of the reality of the things I was experiencing, but to no avail. Her heart towards me was getting colder by the minute.

Chapter 10: A Fisherman's Story

That night I slept very peacefully. Early that next morning, Paul called me. He relayed to me that he had found the perfect church for us. He had set up a meeting with the associate pastor the following Tuesday afternoon. Never did it even cross my mind that it was Sunday morning, and that surely we could have attended a service. When I tell you I was absolutely oblivious to what being a Christian looked like, I mean it. Paul and I got together for coffee and talked profusely about our potential new lives, and what they were supposed to look like. The one thing we both agreed upon is that we could, without any doubt, feel a convicting force within us driving us to change our lifestyles. The power the normal vices that had been part of our lives for years appeared to be broken. The uncontrollable desire to gamble and get drunk that usually haunted our thoughts without reprieve was not there. Can you believe it: that morning we were sitting and drinking coffee! Paul and I drinking coffee! And better yet in the early morning hours, not hung over! To some that may seem to be a trivial transition but to us it was a monumental event. We both also brought a Bible with us. There we were, walking into the local coffee shop, Bibles in hand! What a sight we must have been! Almost everyone in the local community knew who Paul and I were, usually not for a good reason. To see us like this was earth shattering to most. People were so disturbed by seeing us like this that they did not even dare approach us to ask what was going on.

There we sat for hours reading through that book, amazed by the things we read. We were two intellectuals that felt like we had been born into a brand new world at the age of 38. We were not sure what our purpose in life was supposed to be now, except that it definitely was not the life we had been living up to that point. What a humbling time of my life, I felt like I was a young boy being cast into 12 foot waters without any idea how to swim.

There was one comforting fact though that kept me still, prevented me from running away, and was giving me an unrelenting resolve: I knew the greatest lifeguard of all creation was right there with me, and that He would never let me drown! We eventually ended our two man Bible study of sorts and headed to our respective homes. Paul had also shared with me during our talk that morning that he had tried to share what had happened in my basement with his ex-wife, but she told him he was nuts. I shared my condolences, and relayed to him that I hadn't had any better luck with my wife. I continued to encourage him to not let that dissuade him, we had met GOD!

Another evening was spent in my home trying to speak some sense into my wife, although she had quite a different version of what sense was. The frustration of once again so many hours appearing to be fruitless led me back to a one on one session with my Bible as soon as my precious kids were asleep. I had now started to read a little of the Gospels, I had seen that many of the words were in red and I did not know why, but I figured it might be important. So off I went to explore The Gospel of John. I soon realized by deductive logic that the red words must have been spoken by Jesus. I did not know why they were red, so I made a mental note to ask. Maybe the pastor that I was going to meet the coming Tuesday with Paul could answer that for me?

I remember waking up that next Monday morning, as immediately thoughts of God flooded my mind. My normal routine led me to get ready for work; this day though, as I prepared to become a chiropractor for the public yet again, I had no desire to do so. I didn't want to waste another day of my life conducting any function that had nothing, in my opinion, to do with God. As I drove to work I started to pray, or at least I tried to perform what I thought prayer was. I began to talk to God in my car as if he could actually hear me. I did not know what correct prayer was supposed to look like, so I took a chance and just tried to talk to Him.

The theme of my conversation to God was asking Him what I was supposed to do with my life now. Did he still want me to be a doctor? I had no idea as to what was required of me, but I was willing to find out. Not more than five minutes into the conversation I heard Him answer me. This answer was different than any other He had ever given me. He told me to read Matthew 4:19.

I was excited and nervous. God had just given me my first real directive associated with that book, the Bible. On the passenger seat of my car that wonderful book laid on my briefcase. I could have grabbed it and read the instructed passage right then and there, but I was way too nervous to. What did that verse say? More importantly, if it asked me to do something that I did not want to do, then what? This last self-imposed question was quite rhetorical, for I already knew that whatever was being requested of me, I would obey the God of the Universe! Eventually, after grabbing a cup of coffee at the local drive-through, I ventured into my clinic and went straight back to my office. The door was closed and I softly set the Bible on my desk. As I sank into the leather of my office desk chair and reclined, I stared at the book. I knew that once I read what I was about to read there would be no going back. I knew that there could be anything written in that sentence. The God that had written that book was not shy or concerned with people's opinions of Him. I knew it was time to really find out why He had saved me from that dark well and that demon a week ago. My hands were shaking as I opened the cover. I would eventually find the Book of Matthew, and subsequently turn to Chapter four. As my eyes scanned the page, I realized that the verse I was seeking was one of the few verses in red on the page. My heart began to beat faster as my eyes prepared to focus on the words. Again the holy presence filled my office. I could feel that tremendous peace as well. The time had come; God was there in that room with me at my side as I began to read His instructions.

And He said to them: "Follow Me and I will make you fishers of men."

I broke down in tears. I knew God had meant that message for me. He had given me an invitation to come follow Him! I was so humbled by this. I was not really sure what this meant, or what it would look like, but here I came regardless. My answer to Him was a bellowing YES! I began to ponder what it meant to fish for men. I figured it was going to look something like what happened in the basement with Paul. Maybe He would tell me to get together with people and then take over my body, and speak through me each time. That was the best understanding I had at the time. I was so touched by the fact God was even offering me anything to do with Jesus. Those men He walked with 2,000 years ago were so privileged in my sight. Why would He want to have anything like that to do with me? Those were the very words He spoke to the first group of His soon to be disciples back then, and here He was saying those holy words to me. I knew I did not deserve such a privilege, but who was I to argue with Jesus? I was certain the voice inside me that had given me the verse earlier that morning must have been Him. I was so confused as to how exactly Jesus and God were connected, but I did know at that time that they absolutely were.

"Another question I would ask the pastor tomorrow." I thought.
I walked around that day like a kindergartener that had just received his first gold star by the teacher. Each time a patient came in I had less and less desire to be a doctor; all I wanted to do was become this fisher of men. Surely that required training, training that I was sure I was not getting by adjusting backs. Halfway through the day I instructed my office manager that I did not want to

treat any more people that day and to let the other associate doctors in the office treat them. This was met with extreme resistance by her, leading to a quick comprehensive intervention in my office by my entire staff right before lunch. I remember hearing the knocking on the door which led me to offer the usual:

"Come in."

I was clueless that the invitation was being directed to an angry mob on the other side of the door. As the agitated group of people quickly filled my office I sat back in amazement. Then my manager and her assistant began to speak:

"We are worried about you! We do not approve of the new you that is disinterested in this practice, and is always locked away reading the Bible." I think they assumed that this would bring back the old me, and boy were they surprised at my response! I told them that I had met God and that I was going to be a fisher of men. I also told them that my desire to be a doctor, author, or business mogul had faded over the past week. At this, their reaction was that if I did not stop saying these ridiculous things and stop acting this way that they would all quit immediately!

Now you have to understand that I had a very large and successful practice with multiple doctors, so the crowd of employees I was under siege from was formidable. Still, all this being the case, I looked back at them and told them to lock the door on their way out, telling them I was not going to stop reading and talking about the God that I had just met. Truth be told, I was almost hoping they would; I wanted to throw away the practice in that instant and fully devote myself to becoming a fisherman. Unfortunately for me their threat was nothing more than a calculated bluff. They were not concerned about me or my well-being; they were concerned that their job security and income would be affected by the "new me" staying in charge.

Once the bluff was exposed I asked them to please vacate my office because I wanted to spend time alone reading the Bible. This infuriated them even more, but I didn't care at all. No one was going to get me to turn my back on this God that had just revealed Himself to me. I felt like an abandoned child that through a miracle had found his father, and I was not going to give that up at any cost! It was two years later when I began to realize how true that analogy was.

Lunch came and went as page after page of the Bible was explored by this man now wanting to know everything about fishing for men. I thought for sure that the training guide was somewhere in that book. Certainly God had left a manual enclosed for people like me to find since Jesus was gone and back in Heaven. I was astonished at how many times Jesus spoke to people in riddles, not knowing why He did at that time; nonetheless I read on. Then came his interaction with these men He called the Pharisees. I could see a much more serious and angry Jesus as He dealt with this group of people. Truth be told, I knew the Jesus that was there back then was mad at them, and I had already read Revelation, so I knew that the Jesus He had now become was ever powerful and given all power and authority by God the Father. If that Jesus left earth angry at them the newer version of Him was going to come back one day and deal with them. I decided early on that I did not want to be like one of them, and I would try with everything I could to not become one of them. In reality I had no idea at the time what it meant to be a Pharisee. One of the things I did note was that they were very mean to the poor and the weak people in the stories. I also noticed that whenever someone did something bad Pharisees never showed any affinity for mercy. This seemed to make Jesus the angriest. I was trying to take mental notes with every page I read. I thought it was super cool that one Pharisee named Nicodemus snuck out at night to visit Jesus and ask Him questions, I deduced that he snuck out so that his other Pharisee friends would not catch him seeking Jesus. I was intrigued by the dialogue between Nicodemus and Jesus. I read about being born again and about the Kingdom. It all seemed super interesting, but I hardly grasped any of the true meaning, at least not yet.

Eventually I would finish the self- imposed research project and head home. My arrival at home was the usual one: My wife greeted me with a cold shoulder, and a token sarcastic question intent on discovering if I was still a "Jesus guy". As soon as she ascertained I was, she was content to continue shunning me. But, this was not the case with my children. I had never felt as close to my kids as I did after this experience with God. I looked at them with a love I had never had the capacity to have before. They were so precious to me. I could not wait until they were old enough to tell them about Jesus and God the Father. Each night I would tuck them into bed and kiss them goodnight. I would stare at each and every one of them wondering if God would let them be fishermen too.

With my children safe in bed it was once again time to start my personal quest to get my wife to believe in God. Hours were spent yet again in this pursuit, and again the result was the same. You would think that I would become completely surrendered to defeat by now, but that was not the case. There was a determination that had been deposited inside me that would not allow me to do any such thing. But again I invested multiple hours to no avail, so back to the Bible once again. The urge to read Revelation again overtook me. It was like watching the most fascinating movie again, but this time in 3D. The little I had learned from the Gospels had allowed me to better understand The Book of Revelation. At the end I was so overcome with awe once again, and shortly after peaceful sleep was welcomed.

Chapter 11: Did I Ever Tell You I Used to Be Baptist?

My eyes would finally open to the small but sharp rays of early sunlight in from the custom blinds in the bedroom window. It was finally here! It was Tuesday; the day I would finally meet a pastor. I really did not even know what that meant. I just knew that he was a man in charge of a bunch of people in a church. I was really curious to see what a pastor man was like up close and personal. Would he be like the men I was reading about: Peter, John, Paul, and James? Did he have a secret phone line to God like the Bat-phone? Would he be able to read my mind? I could not wait until my 4 pm meeting with him. I felt like a politically aspiring youth granted a private interview with the president. This is all I could think about on my way to work that morning; that and still trying to figure out how to be a fisherman. As I arrived at the office an intervention even greater than the last one was awaiting me. I did not understand how this group of people thought they could convince me to walk away from a relationship with God by threatening to not work at my clinic. It was absurd. Nevertheless, here they were with serious faces and their scrubs in their hands as a gesture they would not even dress for the workday and would leave if I did not yield to their desires. This mutiny was quickly done away with as I left them and told them I was not even interested in seeing patients so I told them to go ahead and leave. With an angry resentment the scrubs became their clothing of choice and off they went to work, defeated again.

Today was such a special day. I was going to be able to speak to what I considered to be a God specialist. This was someone that could answer all my questions, so I better make sure I get them all ready. Maybe I should go read some more of the Bible to try and find some new ones. The morning was slowly passing by, minute by minute until finally 4 pm was approaching. I was so excited; Christmas morning as a child did not compare to the level of raw exhilaration and excitement in me. My friend Paul was also excited, but not as much as me. He made his way to my office by lunch time. We left together to get something to eat before our greatly anticipated encounter. We were like teenage kids getting ready to get in a limo to go pick up our prom dates. Our meal together was spent processing all the possibilities of what this meeting would be like. What were we going to be asked? If he asked us about Christianity, what would we say? What if he asked us about our church background, or where our parents attend church? What if we were too old to join a church, maybe even unable to because we had sinned for too long before deciding to start? We were so nervous we could barely eat. Finally the time had come, and off to the church we went.

The location that Paul had sought out was a church not more than ten minutes from my clinic. I remember pulling in to the parking lot and seeing the large cross over the awning. I felt like I was about to enter a place that was incredibly important. One more silent gaze at each other as we entered the building, as if we could not believe the two of us were actually entering a church, and together none the less. A pleasant older woman met us and offered a warm welcome, after which we were directed to have a seat as she went off to summon the pastor. As she said the very word, pastor, all the questions regarding what this man would be like again began to swirl unrelentingly in my mind. Most of all I wondered if he was also a fisher of men?

Suddenly all the waiting was over. A somewhat tall man a few inches over 6 feet and close to 40 years of age approached us. The man was the anticipated pastor. As he introduced himself as Associate Pastor Harry, he offered us both strong handshakes. My mind began to process what he had just said: He claimed to be an associate pastor, what did that mean? Was he not a real one? Or was he just one in training? Did that mean that he really didn't know God that well yet? Would he still be able to answer our questions? Or would we leave disappointed?

These and so many more were the questions that ran rampant in my thoughts as we walked a short distance to the associate pastor's private office. Harry offered us both a seat and then took his place behind the large mahogany desk.

"Now, what can I do for you gentlemen?"

I had so much to say I didn't know where to start. Paul on the other hand seemed frozen in absolute silence, as if he had already decided to allow me the privilege of breaking the spiritual ice. I started to unleash my story on the man. He was quite attentive as I shared the wild stories trying not to leave out any detail. I could tell though that there was a look of skepticism on his face that as hard as he tried he was not able to hide. After my entire story had been narrated to the audience of one, he got up from his seat and excused himself, saying that he would be right back.

Paul and I looked at each other in a state of wonder. Had I said something wrong? Did he think I was crazy? Maybe he went to talk to God to see what to do with us? I really had no idea what to expect next. Thank God there was not too much time to process all this, as he would quickly return and ask us both to follow him. Where was he taking us? Was there some initiation process that we did not know of that now had to be completed? Was there some sort of application process to be a Christian? I even dared wonder if I was going to have to take a polygraph test to see if I had really met God. But then again I was sure the Pastor knew God, and that God would vouch for me.

I know all these thoughts seem ridiculous now, but believe me, that to me, back then, they were quite real. As we made our way down a much longer hall this time we ended up walking into a much larger office, with a man that seemed a little older, and much shorter than Harry, sitting at a desk covered with papers and pamphlets of sorts. Upon our entry he rose and looked me right in the eyes and greeted me introducing himself as Head Pastor Bill.

I got it. The associate pastor was the screener to weed out the fake Christians, a test of sorts. We must have passed the screening process for here we were in front of the real thing now. Harry relayed to Bill some of my story. I was sure that Bill would be excited to tell me all about the God I had just met, but that was not the case. With a very matter of fact kind of response to my story he offered me a sales pitch on joining the church and then asked Harry to show us around the facility.

What?! This was supposed to be a reunion of two men that both knew God! This was supposed to be an incredible exchange of conversations and stories after a great big hug. Was getting to know God really that small a deal to a pastor? Maybe the excitement was reserved for the fishers of men. I knew that if that was the excitement level to be expected when you became a pastor, then I wanted to stay a fisher of men. As Harry escorted us out of the head pastor's office I must say I was disappointed beyond what words could explain. Why didn't he ask me about God the Father or Jesus? More importantly, why did he not tell me more about Them?

I could not get the mundane and humdrum way we were treated out of my head. I felt as if I had just got off the phone with a telemarketer. Why was God's Pastor so cold? The Jesus of the Bible was never like that. Weren't His Pastors supposed to be like Him? Maybe that church had too many of people like us, and they had no room for me, so they were going to transfer me to a different one for baby Christians. Maybe that was it: I told him I had only met Jesus six days ago. Maybe you needed to have more longevity with God to come here, sort of like a social club or the army. That would have been fine, I just wished he would have told us. Paul, just as he was upon arriving, remained silent, almost as if he was just along for the ride. I then realized that Paul regarded me as the older Christian so he let me lead the way, even though I was only three days older. Harry began showing us the facility. The first thing was the gym, with its full-size basketball court.

I thought it was quite impressive that they had such a beautiful basketball court, but I could not understand why it was in a church. And why was I being shown a sports venue? I felt like I was shopping for an apartment, led by a scrupulous leasing agent. I was really starting to feel weird! I was there to talk about God! Wasn't church supposed to be about Him? I guess my assumptions had been wrong. We were led through the rest of the place, eventually getting to the main auditorium. Here I was being sold on the fact they had a state of the art sound system and a recording booth that sold copies of the sermons in their café after the services. I was so disappointed with the whole thing that I almost just walked out. In my mind I started to ask God why churches were like this? But I did not get an immediate answer. Finally, a boldness came over me and I forced the issue:

"I wanted to ask you some questions about God."

And then: "Can we go back to your office to talk for a bit?"

I could see Harry processing what to respond. I was again disappointed because I could see the main thing on his mind was closing the sale. How disturbing is that?! To top it all off, we were told that we would have to sign a contract if we joined, and that we would be unable to break it once signed. They also were so bold to tell us that they required 10% minimum of all the money we made to be given to the church. They also added that they may ask for tax returns at the end of the year to make sure we were holding up our part of the deal.

This all blew my mind! Why did they need to check my tax returns to see if I was trying to cheat God? Wouldn't God already know if I did such a thing? Wouldn't He inform the pastor? And why were they trying to catch people scamming? Wasn't this a place for people that found God? Weren't these people not supposed to act like that?

He gave us each a copy of the contract and asked us to sign it. I really did not know what to do, so I signed it, without even reading it. I hoped this would now allow me to sit down and finally ask questions about God, since I had now signed an official allegiance to that church and promised by signing it to give them lots of money. My wish was granted, as the three of us gathered around his desk with our Bibles laying before us.

Craig Stasio

Chapter 12 : The Roman Road, and, Why I Never Went to Bible College

I remember receiving my first official Bible study from another person quite vividly. He had titled the teaching "The Roman Road." Harry had called it that because it was a compilation of readings from the Book of Romans. This seemed to be the normal process for a young believer in this church, to help explain to them what had happened to their lives. The story was simple; in essence, as it gave a step by step process of how someone gets "saved." "Saved", a word I had never heard before, at least not in any sort of religious context. The story went something like this: God created humanity, with the first man being named Adam. God also created a woman to be with him named Eve to be his helpmate and wife. God then put them in this incredible garden called Eden full of incredible trees will all sorts of fruits. But in the middle of the garden, there was a tree called the Tree of the Knowledge of Good and Evil. God explicitly told Adam that he could eat from all the trees in the garden, except that one. He also told Adam that if he ever ate from that tree he would die. Harry explained to me that Adam was created to live forever, so by eating from that tree he would be giving up that privilege and choosing instead to be subjected to death. At some point Satan (an angel that was good and then turned evil by rebelling against God) decided to come into the garden in the form of a snake and convinced Eve when she was alone to disobey the command and to eat from the forbidden tree. Not only did Eve do this, but she then took some of that forbidden fruit and convinced Adam to do the same thing. Adam gave in and that is where all of mankind fell into sin. Adam was the forefather of all mankind in God's sight, so he was responsible for what would happen to every man and woman to be born after him. This action was deemed to be rebellion by God, and just as He had promised Adam and Eve; now they would not be allowed to live forever. As a result of their disobedience, God was also forced to banish them from that beautiful garden. But God still loved them so much that He did the most awesome thing: He promised them that one day He would send His own Son to pay for the price of their rebellion in His sight so that He could forgive what they had done. Once His Son had paid for their transgression, they could enter into that forgiveness by believing what He did. The way to pay for Adam's transgression was Jesus being born into the world, and then be crucified. This served as a payment not only for Adam's sin, but the sins of all mankind. The story then led to the point where Jesus would resurrect from death three days later as a sign that sin was completely paid for, and that all mankind had the opportunity to have eternal life again.

Romans said that if "I confessed with my mouth that Jesus was Lord," and "believed in my heart that He rose from the dead" that I would be saved.

My thoughts quickly scavenged to remember if I had done that. "Did I say Jesus was Lord?" I could not recall saying those exact words. "Did it have to be said exactly like that, word for word?" I was so scared I had not said it yet! I am sure you readers can figure out the first thing I did next. The second part of the deal I had already done, I did believe that Jesus rose from the grave after being dead three days. Awesome! I was saved! I could now claim to be a saved person to everybody. I understood that the word saved was in reference to escaping Hell. I no longer was sentenced to go there! That was also part of The Roman Road story; everyone was not only sentenced to physically die as a result of Adam's disobedience, but they would be banished eternally from God upon physical death to a place called Hell. This horrifying place was made by God long ago because, like Adam, angels that were created before us rebelled against God and were cast out of Heaven. There was a similarity to what the angels had done and what Adam had done. So once Adam (representing mankind) did the same thing as the bad angels did, God sent them to the same place as punishment.

Craig was now saved! That place would not get to torture me forever! Again tears erupted from my face. I was so blessed that Jesus and God the Father had allowed me to be pardoned from such a fate. Then I remembered the things I was screaming on my floor in the den the first day of this whole awesome journey. I remembered crying out to God and Jesus to forgive me. I remember understanding and screaming that I knew I deserved to go to Hell. Wow! It was all falling into place. This whole reality had existed the whole time and I never knew it. Every step of my life God was real. Jesus had paid for me to be forgiven 2,000 years ago. And He was trying to catch my attention and get me home to Him. As I pondered this I was flooded with memories of supernatural events from my past that I chalked up as strange coincidences. As I sat there that afternoon I now knew without any doubt that each and every one of those was God reaching out to save me. His patience with me left me undone. How could this all powerful God waste so much time reaching out to me, a rebellious man that kept ignoring His merciful gestures? Worse than that, I was actively allowing myself to be enrolled in Satan's camp with all my rebellious and evil behavior. The horrible things I did in my past I was so ashamed of in that moment. I realized that I had also corrupted so many other people throughout my 38 years in rebellion to God. In the silence of my own mind I asked God to forgive me for all of that. I felt His immediate peace come over me supernaturally. That soothing tingle in my head was also there. Surely this was His "you are forgiven" to me. A feeling of overwhelming gratitude erupted in my soul towards God and Jesus! I could never thank Him enough for what He did for me. But I was going to try and show my gratitude by becoming the best fisher of men that I ever could for Him. I was going to try and show Him my deep heartfelt thankfulness by totally abandoning my life and selling out to do whatever He wanted me to do. I mentally signed the contract with Jesus and begged Him to never let me leave His side again! I was so willing to do anything for Him in that moment.

Ok, The Roman Road teaching had given me a brief explanation of how I was "saved". Now what? I wanted to get to the fisher of men part. I was drafted to play on Jesus' team, so where was the playbook? I wanted to get started in this awesome thing called Christianity. I was ready for the second half of the story to come flowing out of Harry's mouth, but all that followed was a smile and a brief silence. Again I was so disheartened by the experience. Why was I the only apparently passionate and excited person at this meeting?! We were saved! We were no longer going to Hell! There was a whole world of people running around out there that were where I used to be: deceived beyond their wildest nightmares. We had truth, the only way to get out from a horrid fate. I wanted to get my battle gear on and jump into the spiritual fight. I was so angry at Satan and the demons for turning me against this awesome God. I wanted to get out there and start fighting against all the demons alongside Jesus! How could I learn how to fight? Was I just supposed to go out there like people with billboards like: "Repent or perish?" In that moment I gained a respect for people that were out there doing such things. Until that very moment they were nothing more to me than annoying weird people. Now I knew that like me they were people that had met Jesus, and that they were trying to do the best they could to enter the battle field with Jesus.

I couldn't help but to wonder in dismay if that was really all we could do? My King was the resurrected Son of God Almighty! Satan seemed to have supernatural powers, things that he commonly allowed his followers in the occult to use. If the dark side of the force had such powers, what about the good side? Were there no Jedi Knights left in Jesus' army? Where were the Yodas?! I wanted to find a warrior Jesus could use to train me, and I wanted it now. I told myself that after I was trained I would spend my life training others to fight, too. I was so excited at the possibility of receiving such battle training. Surely, Harry knew where to find these fierce warrior generals. So in my Christian innocence I asked him where I could go get this powerful spiritual schooling.

His response was not what I expected. It was almost like he was surprised that I wanted such a thing. After sitting there perplexed for a few seconds he told me that if I really wanted to he could suggest some Bible colleges for me to attend. Now we were getting somewhere, that sounded good to me. Surely a Bible college was a radical place where people lived recklessly like the people of the Bible. I could imagine a whole bunch of passionate people like me living in a dorm together. Instead of keg parties at night they probably went out casting demons out of people or something. I thought that a Bible college must have looked very similar to the school for the mutants in the X-Men movies. I could not wait to meet a spiritual Professor Xavier! I was going to look up the right one for me as soon as I left the meeting. But he called it Bible college. Did that mean I had to go to Bible school and Bible high school first? Was I going to be an oddity starting this whole Bible training at the age of 38? So what. I might have wasted years, but boy was I ready to dig in and get started now! I always hated school; it bored me to death (even medical school). I would sneak out of class all the time and go play golf with my non medical student friends. Funny thing is, I did not know how to play golf, but anything was better than school and boring classes, even looking stupid on a golf course. But now, at the thought of Bible college accepting my application for enrollment, I was beaming with excitement. But I could not help but wonder: What were the pre-requisites for admission? What if I did not qualify? Were there only so many students accepted like a spiritual Harvard? And if that was the case my spiritual C.A.T.'s were probably going to be pathetic; I didn't even have a spiritual G.E.D. Nonetheless I was ready to start filling out applications the minute I got home that night. The meeting would eventually conclude with Harry telling us he was having a men's Bible study tomorrow night, and that we were invited. He told us he hoped to see us there and that it started at 7 pm. I told him I really would like that as I shook his hand and we exited the building. I thought to myself, I don't know if I would actually be able to make it, because I thought I might have already found a real Bible school and enrolled. I really hoped there was one in Michigan, but if not, it didn't matter. I would have went to New-Zealand.

I was surprised that Paul had been so quiet the whole time. Once we entered the car, that silence ceased and we began to have a very colorful discussion of the events. I was surprised that he was not taken aback by the casual aloofness when it came to the head pastor meeting us. And how there was so little apparent zeal in Harry. But I could see that Paul was so caught up in his own situation now that his life was turned upside down that he already had more on his plate than he could handle. He had an ex-wife mocking him, and he had also tried telling his family about the recent events. You can only imagine the resistant responses he received from them. So I decided to let Paul be. Meanwhile, I allowed my mind to wander and roam in the visions of me attending an elite college of God. Maybe this was the new thing now that Jesus was in Heaven. I wished I could have been like Peter or John, getting to spend every waking moment with Jesus as He taught me all the mysteries of the Universe. But hopefully going to Bible college was the same thing. Surely God must have been there all the time. And I was sure there must have been constant manifestations of His supernatural powers as He trained His warriors.

On my ride home that night alone I began to pray, which for me was another way to say I started talking to God. I asked Him where I should go to Bible school. I expected to have a positive and excited response from God. Here I was wanting with all my heart to go to one of His schools, to learn all about Him and His Kingdom. To my dismay not only would He not give me a recommendation, but I could feel that He did not want me going to a Bible school at all! This was extremely disconcerting for me.

"Why not?" I asked myself.

"Why was He not wanting me to?"

"Did I already screw up this whole Christian walk?"

I was so concerned that I had done something really wrong that had disqualified me from this opportunity. I was on an emotional rollercoaster for the next few minutes. Then, as I finally wore myself out with my own emotional tirade, I calmed down. I was ready to actually get an answer from Him. I braced myself for the answer. More importantly, I braced myself for the potential disappointment that might be waiting on the other side of that answer.

It did not take long for a response. God told me He did not want me to go because it would not have been good for me. He also told me He had provided a better way to teach me and grow me up into this fisher of men. I could feel the reassurance of a father in the voice on my inside that talked to me about not going to Bible college. I did not feel so bad or scared now. If God said He had a better way, then He had a better way. I had no idea what that better way would be, but I definitely wanted to find it and get started.

Chapter 13: Speaking on my Father's Behalf

As I got home from the 15-minute drive off I was to battle with the wife once again. This time though, I had more ammunition: I was a member of a church. I might have very well been the newest and most immature member, nonetheless I was an official member as of 30 minutes ago. Surely the fact that I sat down with a pastor and an associate pastor and shared my story should have given it all some credibility in my wife's mind. I was even invited to a Bible study tomorrow night, one that I could attend as my aspirations and dreams of Bible school were quickly squashed by God Himself. Believe it or not, none of this meant anything to her. The conversation would again lead to argument and eventually me bowing out yet again to go back to reading the Bible. I knew though, that tomorrow was still on its way and that we would probably do it all over again.

Wednesday morning began with me awakening earlier than usual, around 5 am. I could feel the presence of God very thick in the bedroom but I did not know why. It was a quiet and peaceful presence but still noticeable, at least to me. I knew without any doubt that God had awakened me, but I did not know why. I slowly wiped my eyes and tried to gather my senses. I laid there in silence, both outside and inside my mind. What a weird feeling, to be woken up by God at 5 am. I did not know what to do, so a laid there and listened. When I say listened I mean inside my own mind. I had learned that if you wanted to hear God speak to you on the inside it helps for us to stop talking. I did the best I could to empty my mind of clutter. Shortly after the small voice inside me that had awakened me, began to speak.

I was compelled to go and get my Bible. I slowly got out of bed and ventured out into the living room turning on the lights. My Bible was in the den, so in I went to gather it, and then I took a seat in the middle of the living room floor. What a wild morning. I did not know that the Bible training that I had sought (and thought I would get at a Bible college) was about to begin all alone in my living room floor. The theme that morning appeared to be centered on the old temple during the time of Jesus. I really had no background at all about this thing called the temple. The voice inside me led me to different parts of the Bible to read all the way from Exodus to Revelation. All themes that in one way or another tied into this temple. I knew what I was being shown that early morning was important, yet I knew I wasn't fully grasping it just yet. I could feel the joy of the small voice that was teaching me. There were so many references to this holy temple... and there seemed to be another one like it in Heaven. The Book of Hebrews talked about one in Heaven that was exactly like the one here, calling the earthly tabernacle a replica of the real one in Heaven. This teaching went on for hours. I felt like a student that had the teacher all to himself. At first I felt like I was not a good student that morning, because I did not fully understand what was being shown to me, at least that is what I felt. On the other hand, I also seemed to feel like as much as this was a teaching moment, it felt like a dad sitting and showing things to his little son, without any expectation of deep accomplishment. The whole situation left me perplexed but excited. The main thing that I took away from the teaching is that the inner most part of the temple was called the Holy of Holies, and God's Spirit lived there with the Ark of the Covenant. And, that no-one except the high priest could go in there, and even that was only once a year. If anyone else dared to enter into the Holy of Holies they died. I also was shown in detail that the first thing that happened when Jesus died is that the veil that divided the Holy Place and the Holy of Holies, also called, the Most Holy Place, was torn in two. I wondered what that meant. If the veil tore why did everyone not die? Shouldn't whatever was inside there come out and killed everyone? Or did

God's Spirit leave when Jesus was dead so it was okay? I really had no idea what it all meant, but I did know God was teaching me.

The bright sun of a full morning eventually captured my mind and alerted me that it was after 9 am and that I needed to get ready for work. Work, who would care about work anymore anyway? I wanted to learn the fisherman part, and now I wanted to know more about this temple and the torn veil in it. How did all the Christians in the world ever find time to do anything else than God stuff? It then baffled me as I started to ponder why Christians at the church I just became a member of only met on Sunday mornings and Wednesday nights? And each time for about 90 minutes only. I would have thought they would meet every day and every night. I just spent over 4 hours with Him by myself and I was hungry for more.

A morning kiss and goodbye to my children and off to work I went. The radio that was normally blazing to Contemporary Top 40 music was left off. The silence in the car helped me to think, and even better to hear the soft voice inside me. I kept pondering the things I had read about the temple and the veil. Twenty-five minutes of pondering and there I was again at my office. As I pulled into the parking lot I stayed in my car for just a bit staring at the building. Was this chiropractic thing even worth doing anymore? Was I just wasting God's time by spending it there instead of being out in the world proclaiming that He was real and that He was good? I did not receive or come to any answers that early morning so in I went.

As I walked into the office, I fully expected yet another intervention by my staff, but to my dismay there was no such thing. I received a couple "good mornings", but they were not given in a pleasant tone at all. I continued to walk towards my office and it hit me that I had still not figured out what to do with the book I had written. Wow! I realized that the one thing that had cannibalized all my time, money, and thoughts over the past four years had not even crossed my mind since Monday, that was a miracle in and of itself. There in my lobby, were posters and hundreds of copies on display for sale. Flyers of my upcoming book signings also filled the countertops of coffee tables in the large waiting area. I looked at all this for a second, and decided that today was not a day that I wanted to spend worrying about my book.

The following week or so was quite interesting, to say the least. Not only did my personal encounters with God intensify, but now these encounters started to happen in a public setting. Now these awesome things began taking place where not only could others witness them, but the experiences started to spiritually capture them as well. This fisherman was finally allowed to throw forth his spiritual net to capture men and woman. The most common manifestation of all this would take place when I would hear God whisper the most bizarre things and nudge me to say them to others. Each time a radical reaction would take place. The words coming out of my mouth would usually answer questions that they were asking in their thoughts. These answers would come in real time, and they would be things that no one could ever possibly know. This supernatural manifestation would open a door for me to speak to them about God. I was so excited! I would jump at the opportunity to share my testimonies with them. I cared very little, if at all, of how insane what I was sharing might appear to be to them. The shock they would succumb to when I shared with them what God told me to say usually made them completely quiet and willing to listen. Sometimes these conversations would last minutes, other times hours. The result of these intense dialogues would always lead to the same crossroad: a choice. Right then and there they would be offered a chance to encounter this God I would tell them about for themselves in a very personal and powerful way. My God never failed to satisfy the willing. Each time the choice was "Yes" I would begin to pray to God to show himself to them, and each time He did just that. Tears of wonder and joy would erupt from within each of them and flow like an emotional, mighty river down their face. I was so privileged to be part of this exchange between God and His new children. Many times they would be left speechless. I always loved to look straight into their eyes after each encounter, to witness the difference that would take place. The dark and cold appearance of their irises and pupils would be taken away, and a bright new set of eyes would be interchanged for them. What a life, watching my God touch and change so many so quickly! I wanted so badly to be able to give them more information about Him, but all I could do was share my testimonies and point them to the Bible for answers. I watched as they would not only change in their facial appearance, but their behavior would undergo an immediate shift. Vices and behaviors that were obviously hostile to God were quickly discarded; drug addictions, alcoholism, and pornography addictions were broken in an instant! No 12-step program, no rehab, no weekly meetings, just immediate freedom! They cried so many tears of joy, knowing within every fiber of their being that they had been completely set free forever from these addictions. These struggles had ruined their lives and destroyed so many of their relationships, but no more. I was so happy! I was a messenger of freedom and hope. I brought a real product with me: life. I would be found countless times left in a prolonged and forceful embrace with a grateful stranger, that by the hands of God was not a stranger any more, but a brother. Watching the power of God sweep over the lives of so many was such a great blessing. It is so hard to describe how privileged I felt being allowed to be part of all this. It was getting to the point that this was all I wanted to do. I began feeling safer and safer with my new God. My confidence was growing with each encounter, as He would always come through and radically touch each person He sent me after. I felt like a salesman with the greatest product ever marketed.

I remember walking into stores and businesses always stopping in the middle of the place to ask Him if there was anyone He wanted me to talk to. I didn't care who it was. And I did not care what it was He wanted me to say. I was just so excited to do anything with my God. I was no different than a little child holding my Father's hand on a great adventure. It was awesome! Most of these people would keep in contact with me after their life changing encounter with God. We would get together and talk for hours, sharing with each other how God invaded every aspect of our lives on a regular basis. We knew we were different in ways we could not ever really understand or convey, but we just were! We felt like aliens transplanted into a world not our own. Even though we had spent our entire lives here before meeting God, it felt like we had just arrived for the first time.

During this time the Lord led me to John Chapter 3. I really began to understand the power of being born again. I was a brand new creation once Jesus had forgiven me, not just a fixed one. I really understood that none of the dark qualities that made up the man I used to be had made their way through the transforming chiasm of salvation. I felt so grateful! I had done so much evil, caused so much pain, and misled so many others to do the same. Not only all that, but I had also been wounded by so many others doing the same to me. But all that mattered nothing now in comparison to the real freedom I had in the Cross. I knew that I was new. I knew also that I had not done any of those horrible things; not the "me" that was in this body now. I very quickly learned to not identify myself with any of my pre-salvation past. I also learned that many would have a problem with this truth. I was amazed at how much people wanted to hold me in contempt as I told them I was a new creation, they were so quick to remind me of all the evil I had done. They were absolutely unwilling to assent to the freedom Jesus' crucifixion had bought me. It was really sad watching people's reactions when their accusations were met with a: "I have been forgiven by God for all that". I realized that there was a dark power fueling their desire to accuse and condemn me. I also figured out very quickly not to listen to the accusatory voices rising up against me. I was disturbed to see how unwilling many people were to the possibility of God actually forgiving a sinner like me. These people limited God's mercy to be available for the casual and minor sinner. But a casual sinner is not what I had been. There was nothing casual in my life, especially not my ability and choices to sin. My attitude had always been that if I was to do something, it would be done in a way that would leave a mark behind. I was quite enthusiastic in all I did, even in sinning. So for those who knew me before I was born again, to hear about the absolute and complete mercy, forgiveness, and freedom I was granted by asking Jesus for grace, it was unsettling. I could see the look in their eyes as they resented me, because I was not paying the price of "what goes around comes around" in my account with God. Time and again, I witnessed the cold hard state of where so many were each time God offered mercy to the sinner. I knew without any doubt that if one of these people were God, that Hell would have been far fuller than it was with my God on the throne making the decisions. Why were people so angry at the mercies of our great God? Didn't they want the same mercy available to them? As much as this bothered me, I did not want it to take up more of my precious time. And yes, my time was very precious now that I had God; each word I spoke as I walked with Him had the potential to set another captive free. Each loving look offered to a stranger could result in drawing an invitation that could ultimately lead to them meeting God. It was so great to have such a feeling of real purpose, after wasting 38 years knowing deep down that my life was empty and void of real meaning.

I remembered learning about the empire of Rome in the years around Jesus' life. They would send messengers before invading a foreign nation to offer people a chance to freely surrender, and assimilate to the Roman culture and empire without resistance. This would result in them being granted Roman citizenship. The smart thing to do was to yield to the Roman forces and avoid a bloody battle they could not possibly win. In a very similar way, I felt as if I was a special messenger sent forth by the Lord ahead of Him. I was sent to alert the people that this King was coming soon, and with Him all of His army to take back the land. I also was allowed to offer them a simple surrender that would result in them also receiving citizenship in the kingdom of the King I was representing. A complete denial of this proposal would not result in an immediate bloodbath and death, but I knew that what was in store for them was far, far worse. Sometimes I would plead with them to repent of their ways, and to embrace the too good to be true offer of salvation Jesus sent me to propose to them. Many times I watched people harden their hearts to God as if they had a right, and a state of entitlement, to do so. I was so scared for them, but even more for myself. In this process I could see the evil nature that can reside in mankind. I observed the hatred and resistance to my loving God, knowing that all of us are more than capable to end up in that place. I clearly remember an instance where in my car, as I was leaving from preaching to one of these people who had rejected, crying out to God to keep me from becoming like that! I screamed through cascading tears for Him to never allow me to hate Him or turn on Him. I also cried out to Him to never let me be deceived in that manner. It was a desperate, frantic prayer in the solitude of my Jeep. I knew my creator was listening, and I knew He would answer me. Like a bright ray of sunlight piercing the morning overcast of the greyest sky, so were the words spoken on the inside of me amidst the tears and pleas.

"You will die for me."

My tears erupted even more than before! God had again been faithful to His servant's cries for help. I felt so safe. My life was His, and now even my death was, too! I did not have to worry anymore! It is quite unusual, I know, to rejoice at the message of one's death. But, where I was in those moments, fearful that one day I might betray my awesome God, those words brought nothing but freedom and joy! I could set this fear aside, and focus on spending my life to serve my King in peace, knowing that at the end of it I would not be standing before Him as an enemy. Of all the words God has spoken to me in the last nine years, none have ever touched my heart as intimately as the ones telling me I would die for Him. I wanted to honor God with all I had, even my last breath. I wanted my last words on this earth do be a declaration of my loyalty to my Savior, to the Majesty of His being. I was so grateful that I was allowed to be His.

Another time I was driving and I was overcome by deep emotions, I knew that God was right there in the midst of my thoughts, asking me to share with Him why I was so emotional. My answer to Him was a simple and honest one:

"I don't know why You would even talk to me?!"

I knew I was so unworthy of the things of my King. I did not deserve to hear the precious voice and words of God. Every word He spoke to me was more precious than anything I had ever held. I knew that if He ever stopped talking to me I would just want to die. I felt very vulnerable talking to Him about my feelings in regards to Him talking to me. But I had developed a real relationship of trust with Him. We had real intimacy, me and God. We could talk about anything, He was my best friend, and He still is. I had no hidden thoughts or feeling from Him, and I did not want to, either. I wanted Him imbedded in every part of my being and my soul. I never wanted anything to come between us; this was a relationship I knew I could not live without. It always baffled me when God would ask me what I was thinking about, because I knew He already knew. I also knew that if He asked me, that He really cared about me answering. It is so wonderful to have such a real relationship forged from the greatest power in all of creation: love. After telling God that I could not understand why He would spend any of His time talking to someone like me, he answered:

"I love you, son."

Four words that pierced me deeper than any sword ever could, I was undone to my very core. I violently cried sincere tears. These tears seemed to free a wounded part of me so deep, that I just allowed the overwhelming process to unfold. I knew He meant what He said. He loved me; me, the broken but now redeemed man before Him. Me, the horrid sinner, now made clean. But, even more, I was not a slave, but He dared to call me a son. I had wanted those words to be spoken over my life in truth ever since my childhood. Being abandoned by my biological father at the age of one had left such a deep void in me, so deep I was never courageous enough to allow myself to fully experience the pain. But there I was in my car, again allowing God to open the barricaded door to a room of severe pain deep in my heart. My little hand rested on His large and powerful one, as together we turned the knob to open the door. He wanted me to open it with Him, knowing that I was safe because He was with me. I trusted Him, and turned the knob opening myself up to experience the pain. But God wanted to take the pain from me. He instead flooded healing and love into that previously dark and wounded part of me. I felt as if a missing part of my very being was restored to me. I felt more complete than I ever had. I replayed the words in my mind and in my heart over and over as I pulled the car over by the side of the road. I was unable to drive due to the tears interfering with my ability to see clearly.

"Son": what a powerful word to me. I dared to believe it, I really did. I took it in with a guarded voracity, making it mine forever. I thanked God so many times that day for allowing me the Honor of being His son. I pleaded with Him again to keep me from ever not wanting to be His son, or from doing anything that would cast me out of His house. After Him I knew there would never be another that could be my Father. I wanted to hold on to this One, the only real One with everything I had within me. Again, as I felt somewhat scared, even horrified, at the thought of ever being cast away from my new Father, I pleaded with Him to keep me His forever. At this He again reminded me that I was going to die for Him. Never had the thought of death brought such complete peace. Close to an hour was spent next to the ditch on the side of the road assimilating the truth that God Loved me, and that He had made me His son. I was changed forever by this revelation, this great personal truth. This was so precious to me that I kept it all to myself for a while. I imagine that if people were angry that He forgave me, they would really be upset that He loved me, and made me His son. It was so amazing to me to now pray to God as my Father. Not THE Father, but MY Father! He was really mine! Heaven would allow me entrance as a son, not a stranger or vagabond. I dared to believe He actually took pleasure in me coming into His throne room to talk to Him. I was not going to come to him like a skittish cat anymore. I was going to completely throw myself into this new reality. I was not willing to let this truth escape me for a second. I thought of how much joy I had each time my little girl or my sons ran toward me. I dared to believe that is how my Father felt when I came to Him. I believed His arms opened to take me in. I believed His lap was always open to me; no matter what else was happening in Heaven, His lap was open for me. All the angels of Heaven could be caught in a frenzy before His throne, but my Father would not ignore me if I came to seek Him. I was undone. I wanted with all my heart to look straight into His eyes and cry myself to sleep as I thanked Him for loving me. His Son had made that a truth to me more than anything else ever could. That cross and His crucifixion made me believe my Father meant what He said. What a priceless treasure, God as my real Father. I knew one day I would enter His heaven and that it would also be mine forever. I would one day be home in my Father's house. As much as I wanted to go home and be with Him then, I knew He had things He wanted me to do here with Him first. I wanted so desperately to be a son that made Him proud. I was willing, ever so willing, to do, to go, or to become, anything He wanted. I wanted to pour my life out before his feet as a gesture of the deepest gratitude I have ever experienced. What a change in my prayer life. What a change in my thoughts toward myself. All the shame of being a bastard child washed away. All the hopelessness and abandonment erased forever. No adoption papers were signed in Heaven, for I was not adopted as I was; I was born again as His son. I was of His bloodline now. I belonged to Him. But more than all that: He belonged to me! He was my Father, and He would be forever. That day did things inside of me that I could never fully express in thousands of pages, or even countless books. But now every day of my life shows a little more of what happened to me back then on that glorious day.

Chapter 14: My God Uses the Telephone

I remember one of the craziest days in my first years of walking with God. I had been born again less than a year. Two of the scariest days of my life had just passed by. I had been unable to hear my Father's voice for two days straight. This brought a panic and fear to me like nothing else ever could back then. I had tried everything I knew to do to hear Him, but all that was to no avail. I was close to catatonic. Countless discouraging, and even horrifying, thoughts rampaged in my mind and my heart.

"Had I done something to anger my Father?"

"Had I offended Him without knowing it, causing Him to cast me away?"

"Was I now going back to Hell again?"

"If I had done something, I would change and beg for forgiveness! I just needed to hear Him speak it to me!"

The people around me had noticed the rapid decay of my demeanor and my emotional status as the 48 hours of silence pounded against my heart. I finally walked into my back office in the clinic in the middle that workday. My knees bent once again as my body was lowered towards the tan carpet. My prayer was lifted with a voice that crackled through the tears. This was a prayer that I will never forget. I poured out myself before my God like never before. I began that monumental prayer by asking Jesus to please take from me four very specific things that I was struggling with. I also told Him that I was being overcome by an anxiety that I knew was not from Him, and I asked Him to take that from me as well. I followed that by telling Jesus that I knew He came to give me His peace. I declared that I was going to accept that peace by Faith. My prayer then turned to my Father: I expressed my fear that I was not sure if I was still His son, and that I had not heard His voice in two days. I told Him that if I was no longer His that I didn't care if I lived or died anymore, and to do whatever He wanted with me. I pleaded with Him to please let me know I was still His! This prayer was sealed with a: "In Jesus' Name".

Slowly I rose again to my feet, and looked straight up at the ceiling as if to look to Heaven to show my desperate state and tears to my Father. After this, still emotionally distraught, I made my way back to my office having not heard any response as of yet.

You have to understand that talking to God my Father and hearing from Him was more important to me than the very air I breathed. The fact I could not hear His voice scared me in ways nothing else could. I was desperate to hear Him. I wanted closure. I needed to know the truth at any cost. I was terrified at the thought that perhaps I had, in some way, ruined my relationship with Him.

As I entered the office I sat at one of the large desks in the middle of the room. I had left my cell phone resting on the countertop to my right. I folded my arms and rested my head in between them as I resigned to my fate. My silent stare caught the eyes of my new wife Danielle, a story you will shortly hear of. She felt compassion for me, knowing how badly I was hurting not hearing the voice of my Father. She did not know what to do to help me, but I know she was praying to the one that did. I could feel the silence in my heart, as no words from within had been spoken by my Father yet. I had no idea where I would go from there. What was I supposed to do without the leading of my Father? I did not know, and even more, I did not care. A life without God to me was a useless existence. Not more than three minutes transpired as the silence around me was invaded by the ringing of my cell phone. I slowly picked it up to look at the number calling me. The three digit prefix alerted me to the fact that the call was originating from out of state. This was a three-digit area code that I did not recognize, and it was a number

I did not know. I was sure that it was nothing more than one of the countless vendors or creditors that harassed me on a daily basis. My normal reaction to such an unknown caller was always to silence the ringer, and put the phone away, allowing them to leave a message that I would later check at my convenience. Somehow, this time I felt an overpowering need to answer this strange call, so I did.

"Hello?"

A southern woman's voice began to speak from the other end:

"Is this Craig?"

I now, more than before, thought it was a telemarketer, but something inside me did not let me discard the call just yet:

"Yes, it is. Who is this?"

I anxiously waited for a response that would hopefully shed light on this strange call.

"My name is Ms. Johnson from the Inspiration network, can I pray with you?"

Never had I gotten a call from a stranger asking me if they could pray with me. What was I supposed to say? I was desperate, and willing to do anything to hear my Father's voice again. So what could it hurt for a stranger to pray for me over the phone? The funny thing was that I really did not spend a lot of thought trying to figure out who she was, or how she had gotten my number. So I gave her a simple answer of yes, granting her permission in the spirit to pray for me. What was to follow has changed me forever.

"Craig, the Lord Jesus says that He has heard your cry, and that He will take the four things that are tormenting you." As if this was not crazy enough, she named the exact four things that I had just prayed about on the floor of my back office.

She then went on to pray:

"The Lord also says that the anxiety that has been tormenting you is not from Him, and he will take that too. He also says that He will give you His peace."

By this point she completely had my undivided attention! It was undeniable that God had sent this woman to speak to me! I was all ears, and all heart! The woman then shifted the attention from Jesus to the Father: "And Craig, the Father says that the devil has been coming after you for two days to make you believe that you are not His son, but that He is faithful to complete the work He began in you."

I could almost feel the smile erupt on her face as she was excited to be used by our common Father. She then ended the conversation with a simple:

"God bless you and goodbye."

I stared at the phone as I slowly put it back on top of the desk. My wife had watched the look in my eyes change, and my demeanor be transformed as the phone call transpired. I looked intently into her eyes but spoke no words to her. I rose silently from my desk, and walked towards my office once again. The door would again close, and my knees would feel the rugged carpet again. My kneeling lasted only an instant, as I quickly threw myself on the floor and wept like a baby, flooded with new hope and joy! I thanked my Father and Jesus for hearing my cries, and for answering me. More importantly, I thanked God for His faithfulness, and His promise to complete the work He started in me. I wept for close to half an hour. I felt life and purpose again flood my being. I had learned an important lesson that day: do not allow circumstances to dictate the reality of God's promises towards me. He had been faithful all along. I was actually encouraged that Satan had spent time attacking me, and my position as God's son, because it only strengthened my faith in my Father and Jesus's salvation for me. What a phone call! What an awesome god! God called me on the phone! My face glowed for days as a result of this great experience, the same way it is now as I recall and relay this story to you.

Chapter 15: The Lord God said "It is not good for the man to be alone..."

Now I will tell you of my new wife, Danielle. This is where my story, and my life, gets even more controversial, if you can even believe that is possible. I spent the first four months after I was born again with my now ex-wife. There were countless supernatural experiences shared with her as God hi-jacked my life, and tried to recruit her to His Kingdom as well. None of these radical events were able to pierce her heart and turn her to Jesus. I spent days and nights pleading with that woman to accept Jesus, and to believe that the God of the universe had recruited me for a mission in His name. All of these attempts were met with an unfortunate level of anger and disgust. I remember crying so many tears to God as I shared the rejection and hurt my marriage to her had caused and was still causing me. I pleaded with God to do whatever it took to save her, but I could only see her turning further and further away from Him. One day right around Christmas I ran into a woman that I had vaguely known up to that point, Danielle. She was a casual acquaintance, and had sent me a simple Christmas card as a token of a holiday gesture of kindness. The next time I saw her I walked up to her and we embraced each other in a simple hug of friendship. I thanked her for the nice Christmas card. What appeared to be a simple interaction was one forged in Heaven that would have great and wonderful implications for the both of us. As I began to pull away from this friendly hug I heard a resounding voice inside me that I knew with certainty was my Father:

"This is your wife!"

I was shocked. I broke away from Danielle, almost so that I could get a look at her face to see if she had heard the voice, too. She seemed unaffected by the whole event. I knew at that point that I was the only one to hear what God had just said. Now, you have to understand that I was a baby believer, only two months born again. I knew that God did not condone polygamy, and I also knew He was not an advocate of divorce. Both of these things were learned reading the red letters in the Gospels. I did not know what to do with the message I had just heard. I remember staring awkwardly at Danielle in silence trying to rapidly process this event. I did not know if there was something that I had to do or say, but I did not hear anything so I did nothing in that very moment, at least, nothing Danielle would notice. I asked her to have coffee with me one day. I figured it was wise to try and set up another interaction between the two of us. And I would use whatever time available between now and then to ask God what to do. She cautiously agreed. We then went on our own ways.

My wife? How was this Danielle my wife? What about the one I already had? I was caught up in an emotional whirlwind layered with countless questions. I quickly ran to the two minister ladies that I was learning from, and relayed the whole story to them. Their apparent surprise could not be hidden from their expressions. They did not know what to say to me. They tried to dissuade me from believing that God would ever speak such a thing to me. I was so freaked out! I believed with all of my being that the voice who spoke to me was God. If that voice was not God what was I supposed to do now? That had been the voice to guide me all along from the very moment that I was born again. If that was not God, then I was in some serious trouble. I trusted God had brought these two women to help me, but I also knew that same voice had told me Danielle was my wife. After many frustrating hours of conversation that bore no simple answer or closure, I departed from the girls' house, and headed home. I talked to God and asked Him to help me understand, and to help me to do whatever His will was in this situation. I felt peace again in the car, and I knew that He had heard, and that help was on the way. I then, in faith, did a simple act to show I believed what I heard. I had saved Danielle's phone number in my cell phone as a new contact after she agreed to go out for coffee in a few days. Instead of her name to accompany the new number I erased Danielle and wrote "Future Wife" in its place. This was a strong stand in what I believed I had just heard.

As I got home, my then present wife was as hostile as ever towards me. I dared not even bring up what I had just heard. This night was probably strange to her, because instead of debating with her about the reality of Jesus or my new life, I just quietly went to bed. I laid there contemplating what it would be like to have Danielle as a wife, knowing one thing for certain: that if God was telling me that she was called by Him to be my wife, then she was the perfect wife for me, and that I could not find anyone better. The awkward emotions would give way to a peaceful night of sleep. Two or three days later, Danielle and I went out for our first real conversation. She had no idea what to expect from me, as I seemed really interested in her company, and I had initiated the meeting for coffee. A fancy Italian restaurant was the location of this first talk; I did not know what to say to her. I figured if she really was going to be my wife, that she already knew Jesus or if not she would soon meet Him, too. I knew that God wanted a husband and wife-to-be on one accord, and that they were to be evenly yoked together. I quickly figured that I would share my recent testimony of my salvation experience, and see how she responded. I excitedly expressed my desire to share an awesome story with her, inquiring about her willingness to listen. Her response was quite unique: "You can tell me whatever you want, just as long as you do not proselytize to me."

I really had never had heard that word before, so I assumed that talking about my encounter with God was open game. I did not know that word was actually spoken to dissuade me from sharing my testimony. To this day I am glad that I did not know the meaning of that word. My story unfolded with zeal and a high level of excitement. I could see the anger and disgust overflow from within Danielle as I continued with my story. I could not understand what this meant. I thought that in order for her to be my wife, surely she would also choose to follow Jesus. I was so overcome with emotions and unanswered questions, but I did not detour from my intention to completely share my testimony.

The dinner unfolded as I could notice both Danielle and our waitress rolling their eyes in disdain at me. After a most uncomfortable dinner we would head back to my car. I had met Danielle at a common place and then drove her to the restaurant. We quickly arrived back at the parking lot that was now empty of all other cars than hers. I pulled next to her car, and the soft voice inside me began to again bellow like a howling wind. I felt an aggressive push from God to begin to share the things I was hearing about Danielle's childhood, specifically an event from when she was five years old. It was an emotionally traumatizing event that no one knew but her... and now me. She broke down in tears. She was overcome by the return of all the emotions attached to the event. She did not understand how I knew these things in her heart, and it really freaked her out.

The night would end with Danielle telling me I was weird and creepy, and that she was not sure she ever wanted to hang out with me again. She then told me not to contact her for at least two weeks. I was sad, but I agreed to her request. We parted ways, and again I headed home. I was very confused as to the outcome of the night. This was supposed to be my Christian wife. There was no evidence at all that this woman would ever want anything to do with the God that now meant everything to me. But again I reached deep within me to grab hold of the learned reality that despite my circumstances, God knew what He was doing, and that He was faithful to complete His promises. That was exactly what this was in my heart: a promise. Danielle would one day call me husband, and I would call her my bride. I was pretty shook up as I began to talk to my Father, as again we were alone in the car. I told Him that it was going to be very hard to not call her for two whole weeks. I also shared with him that I was scared that another man might snatch her up in that time and steal her away from me. I also shared with Him the fear of her being intimate with another man in that time. I knew she had at least one boyfriend, and maybe more. I was shaken inside at the thought of another man being intimate with Danielle, my wife. That's right, she wanted nothing to do with me that cold winter night, but that did not matter, in my mind and my heart she was my wife-to-be. Nothing could ever change that. I knew it was absolute truth because my Father had spoken it to me. I was shaken the most because I assumed she would spend some of the next two weeks with another man. I told God that this would hurt me really badly, and that I did not know if I could bear it, but He told me to trust Him. I took the emotional calendar in my heart and clipped the next two weeks shut. I took in a deep breath, and trusted my Father again. I asked Him if He could please keep me busy during that time so that I could have my mind focused on other things so that I would not miss her. I could feel him smile and agree.

It was really hard for me to trust women. I had been road kill to adultery and infidelity so many times that I no longer believed in monogamy. But now I was a new creation, one that was born into a reality where faithfulness is real. I trusted that Danielle would one day prove that the Godly quality of faithfulness could exist in a wife. I also was set on proving that it could also exist in a husband, the one I wanted to be one day to her. I decided to give my heart to God to guard for the next two weeks, and to get back to fishing for men. During that two week waiting period a great new event was to take place in my life. I had asked my Father to keep me busy to help keep my mind off of Danielle--little did I know what He had in store for me.

Chapter 16: ...And Then I Wasn't Baptist Any More.

In the following days, I spent many evenings and hours at the house of my Baptist pastor, trying to learn all I could about my new life as a son of God. I also attended any and every Bible study that I heard about; I even tried to start some of my own. At one of these studies in his living room I stumbled across scripture that talked about a commonly repeated topic: The Holy Spirit. I asked the associate pastor about the Holy Spirit. His answer was evasive and unfulfilling. He said that I already had it: the Holy Spirit. I asked him to elaborate on this, but again the answers were evasive and vague. I then went home determined to learn more about the topic. I looked up the words Holy Spirit in the glossary at the end of my Bible and read each passage where it was used. I read about the wild things that were done by the Holy Spirit. I also came to the understanding that He was a person, not a thing. Why hadn't the Father introduced me to the Holy Spirit yet? I did not understand. Jesus was his son, and also God too, but how did the Holy Spirit fit in to all this?

I read on and on. I read in the Book of Acts that the Holy Spirit killed two people, Ananias and Sapphira, for lying to Him. He had my attention now. I was really scared of Him, but at the same time I could feel the soft voice of God inside me, nudging me to go further, and not to fear. I read in Genesis how the Holy Spirit hovered over all creation preparing to bring life forward. He was here on the earth in the beginning...wow. I then was enthralled reading about Jesus talking to His disciples about the Holy Spirit. Telling them that one day He would leave the earth and send the Holy Spirit to be with them, but not only with them, He would be IN them. God inside me? How did that work out? Was He already in me? The voice of God that spoke to me came from inside me, so maybe He was already there...I was so overwhelmed. I read on to when Jesus was water baptized, and the Holy Spirit descended upon Him. It was obvious to me that right after this Satan came after Him in the desert to attack Him. But, it was also evident to me that all the miracles Jesus did began after the Holy Spirit paired up with Him. The importance of the Holy Spirit was becoming more and more evident to me as I read on. Hours transpired as I searched and researched for any and all information I could find in the Bible about the Holy Spirit.

I eventually came upon the scriptures in the beginning of the first chapter of the Book of Acts. I read as Jesus told His Disciples to go and wait somewhere. He told them that they would be endued with power when the Holy Spirit came upon them. What did endued mean? I looked into it and decided that I wanted to be endued with power too. I asked God if I was allowed to be a disciple, too. Did I have to go to a second or third floor room somewhere and pray for days to get it? I wanted to find the pattern or the exact way one was supposed to get the Holy Spirit. I continued to read on in Acts and saw all the cool things that happened at the hands of The Holy Spirit.

Then, I finally came across the mentioning of the Gifts of the Holy Spirit: prophecy, words of knowledge and wisdom, faith, working of miracles, diverse tongues, interpretation of tongues, and finally distinguishing of spirits. I was sold on the Holy Spirit! I wanted Him in me too! I felt like God had told me that I was allowed to be a disciple too, and if I was going to be one, I wanted to be a real one. I wanted to have the Holy Spirit in me in this crazy new life awaiting me. I eventually ended up in the Gospel of Luke, Chapter 11, verses 9-15. This passage of scripture simply said that if I asked the Father for the Holy Spirit, then He would Give Him to me to live inside me. I was excited! But, I was also a little scared. I did not want to do anything wrong, because I read about what the Holy Spirit did when people made Him angry. I did not want to have any assumptions about what I was allowed to do or ask for until I had more clarity.

I had invited three pastors and a youth pastor to my house for pizza, pop, and fellowship the next day. I figured I could wait until the next day to ask more questions about the Holy Spirit (now that I was somewhat educated on the topic from reading all I had in the Bible about Him). Thoughts of the Holy Spirit ran wild in my mind that whole night as I tried to fall asleep. I was so excited about this new thing, I didn't even notice at the time how much it took my mind off of Danielle, like I had prayed for; what an awesome and faithful Father.

The next evening would come quickly, and there I was with three pastors and the youth pastor walking around with paper plates filled with pizza and plastic cups bearing Coke and Sprite. I had provided my part to this community venture, now I wanted the pastors to provide me what I wanted from this meeting: answers. I bluntly positioned myself in the midst of all of them and loudly shared with them that I had done some extensive research the day before about the Holy Spirit, and that I had some more specific questions to pose to them. I could see them all become quite squeamish, but that was not going to detour me. I shared what I had read, and then showed them that Jesus said to ask the Father for the Holy Spirit in Luke Chapter 11. I also showed them in Acts 8:9-18 that new born again believers in Samaria did not have the Holy Spirit until Peter and John came to them and laid hands on them, praying for them to receive the Holy Spirit. I also showed them that in Acts Chapter 19 that the Apostle Paul came across twelve believers and asked them if they had received the Holy Spirit yet, and their response was that they did not even know there was a Holy Spirit. Paul then taught them, laid his hands on them, and prayed for them to get the Holy Spirit, and they did! The small crowd in my kitchen now seemed to get quieter, and even more uncomfortable.

It was then that I delivered the question that seemed to unravel them at their core. I asked them what I had to do to speak in the tongues that scripture talked about. All the scriptures I read showed a common manifestation that all the people that received the Holy Spirit had: they spoke in tongues immediately after receiving the Holy Spirit. Tongues, the apparent no-no word in the Baptist circuit. How was I supposed to know this?! I had just poked the sleeping giant inside the Baptist pastors there. A heated conversation broke out amongst them. The fun thing is that the two woman ministers that were also mentoring me had shown up at my house, too. I could see the disdain the Baptist pastors had towards them. To tell you the truth, I was quite unsettled by the demeanor and behavior these men showed towards these Godly women. The debate about the Holy Spirit and tongues raged on between them. Conflicting points of view were discussed, and then argued over, eventually leading to some of the most heated exchanges I had ever witnessed as a Christian. I made my way out from among them and stood off to the side by myself. I was frustrated with them. All I wanted to know was how to get the Holy Spirit and tongues! It was in that moment as the intense debate echoed in my home that I broke my silence with a loud plea:

"Father, they will not help me get the Holy Spirit, will you, please?"

They heard my sincere plea to God the Father right in front of them. They looked at me with even more disdain, almost as if they were appalled by the fact that I thought I could talk to my Father like that. I, on the other hand, knew that my Father had heard, and that He would most certainly help me. The uncomfortable atmosphere prompted me to ask them all to leave my home. I was relieved when the house was mine and my God's again. I listened to see if His answer to my request was available yet. In that very moment my phone rang. Another young woman that I had met after being a Christian was calling to invite me to a church service the following morning at 7 am. She said that she felt God wanted her to take me there. I was excited. Anytime God had someone call me, or invite me to something, great things happened. I wondered if this had anything to do with my recent request. I agreed to go with her, and later that night I asked the two woman ministers that were helping me to come as well, and they agreed.

It was barely light out as I began to dress myself for church after a hot early morning shower. I was quite excited to see what was going to happen. I drove to meet the woman and got into the back seat of their car. Another great adventure had begun. They drove me about twenty minutes away from my house to a huge church complex that looked like a medieval monastery. Later on I found out that it used to be exactly that. I exited the car with even more excitement then when I entered it. I could see a very large crowd coming in from all sides of the building. I also noted that more than 90% of the patrons were African American. I was intrigued. I entered the large doors and was immediately greeted by some incredibly friendly people. They seemed far more sincere in their joy than the people at the Baptist church. I shook some friendly hands, and proceeded into a great auditorium. Thousands of people were there singing to God, my God. I was so happy to see this, I began to tear up. They loved my Father, too. Thirty minutes of wonderful songs praised our God and brought such a sense of peace into that building I felt like I never wanted to leave. Then the teaching: a comprehensive overview of the coming tribulation, a perfect teaching to keep my attention. After this was the typical offering plates, and the greeting of your pew neighbors. I thought this was all cool and great, but still felt somewhat unsatisfied. I knew that if God had set up this venture, then something greater than what I had seen was still coming.

It was then that the crowd quieted down and the pastor began to speak again. He started to share the simple message of salvation through Jesus and asked anyone in the crowd that did not know Jesus to come forward if they wanted to know Him, and have Him forgive their sins. I was so happy to see so many rising from their seats, and head towards that large podium. After this call for salvation the pastor began to say that anyone who wanted the Holy Spirit Baptism with the evidence of speaking in tongues to come forward as well. What?! Did I really just hear that?! YES, YES, YES, ME! I grabbed one of the pastor ladies and pulled them with me to go to the pulpit. I felt like she was my mom, and that she would keep me safe from whatever might go wrong. She smiled and laughed as my childhood zeal and manly body dragged her rapidly to the front row. Shortly after, we were escorted to a separate room where people were going to pray for us to receive the Holy Spirit.

They began reading scripture about the Holy Spirit and how to receive Him. I remembered all the verses; I had read them over and over in the last 48 hours. This was awesome! God was so faithful to me! They eventually came to Luke Chapter 11 verses 9-15: if we asked the Father for the Holy Spirit, He would give Him to us. I was excited beyond what words could describe. They told us that if we asked we would receive the Holy Spirit, and that then we could speak in tongues. Not more than 10 seconds later I asked the Father for the Holy Spirit. I began to feel so connected to my God, just me and Him. Even though the room was full of many others, that moment was just mine and His.

I then came to the moment of truth: speaking in tongues. I was tired of waiting. I wanted to be able to have this supernatural spiritual gift with everything in me. So in a great leap of faith I closed my eyes and asked God to allow me to have the gift. I told Him that I believed Him when He wrote in the Bible that if I asked for the Holy Spirit He would give it to me, and I knew that He was not a deceiver so: here I came, ready or not. I opened my mouth and began to talk while meditating on my great God. Before I knew it I was captivated by the very words coming out of my mouth. Tongues! Real Tongues! I was speaking in a language I did not know or understand. One of the pastors there smiled as he noticed me doing this and walked over and put his hand on my chest. As he did the tongues became louder and his smile grew brighter. I was so very happy. I had the Holy Spirit in me! I could speak in tongues! I was not only a fisher of men, but now I was a disciple, too! Could life get any better than this? As I look back on all of these events I note two things: First, I was completely distracted from thoughts of Danielle, and second, I really believe I had received the Holy Spirit the day I was born again, I just did not know it.

The following day I went to the Baptist pastor's Bible study with a level of excitement that could not be contained. I was so excited to show him that now I was a disciple too. And, that I could finally help him believe that the Holy Spirit Baptism was real, and so was our ability as Christians to speak in tongues. To my surprise, the greeting and response that I would receive from him and his small home gathered congregation was brutal. I felt a level of rejection I thought I never would have to experience from another believer. They were angry and resentful towards me, as I shared my incredible story from the previous day. They said things to me that I never want to repeat. Calling me names and referring to my experience as something I never want to hear again. I was left speechless and wounded. I could not understand how people that read the same Bible and claimed to know the same Father were so against the experience I just had with the Holy Spirit. They eventually asked me to leave their house. My best friend Paul happened to also be at that Bible study. I aggressively encouraged him to leave with me, explaining that I had a real experience with God and that he could, too. I told him not to listen to what they were saying, and that they were deceiving him about this great truth. I could see it in his eyes, the great divide of his own thoughts and will. He was processing who to stand with, me or them. Sadly the choice was one that would leave us void of any communication for about a year. But, that was a small price to pay to stand on the side of truth. I was fully convinced it was worth it to be a vessel that now contained the Holy Spirit, not to mention I could speak in tongues now!

The following days would be filled with me getting to know the Holy Spirit that lived in me. I spent countless hours speaking in tongues. I really did not understand the importance of this, but I knew that it really was important for me, so I did it. It was such an encouraging thing, a supernatural ability to further demonstrate the reality of my new life, and my new King. I could feel myself getting spiritually stronger and more aware as I continued to speak in tongues. I began to ask God to show me the importance of these tongues in the Bible. His answer came quickly as he led me to verses in I Corinthians and Ephesians explaining that this is how we grew and learned the deep spiritual things of His Kingdom. It was also a way to engage in spiritual warfare. I was even more resolved now to use my new gift. The next week and a half would pass quickly.

Chapter 17: The Lord Says His Word Has Set You Free

There I was two weeks from my last encounter with Danielle. I was allowed to call her again. I asked God how to proceed, I felt like He wanted me to pursue her again, but I was not exactly sure how. It was then that the voice inside me gave me the idea of getting two tickets to a hockey game and to invite her. I called one of my vendors and was able to obtain two premier tickets. I then called the woman I was resolved to marry, and requested her company at the game. She refused at first, but after repeated attempts to get her to come she finally caved in and agreed. We drove to downtown Detroit, and parked in the Valet at the local casino close to the arena. Prior to my salvation I frequented that establishment daily and so I had earned a V.I.P. parking pass. But now the only business I was willing to do there was park so I could walk my future wife to the hockey game in comfort. I could see her mind race as I parked in the casino and everyone there knew me by name. She could not put together a man who claimed to know Jesus, but was a well-known entity at a casino. Nevertheless, she proceeded to the game with me. I tried to listen to God as to exactly what to say to her. We entered the arena and found our premier seats. She was excited to see the quality of seats we had, while I was excited to see her there with me. I imagined waking up next to her one day with my arms wrapped around her as my wife. I did not know how God was going to pull this off, but I was excited and sure that He was going to. The game began and Danielle started to watch the frenzied pace on the ice, while all I wanted to watch was her. It was not even the end of the first period when I asked her to leave the game and go sit somewhere so that we could talk. She was very surprised at this, but agreed anyway.

A local Coney Island diner is the place we ended up. We spent hours getting to know each other in the late hours of that night in the small, secluded booth. The night would again come to an end as I dropped her off at her car, as I had the previous time. This time was different than the last one, on this occasion there was no weird exchange of words, or supernatural revelations from her youth, just a sincere hug and a goodbye. I was grateful that this time there was no disclaimer that would forbid me from contacting her for a determined amount of time. I could tell that she was still confused by me and my demeanor, but she still appeared to be drawn to me and unable to understand why. I trusted God that whatever was necessary to bring this new marital relationship to pass, He would do it. I drove away this time more encouraged and less demonized than I had on our last adventure.

Upon my return to my home I was again greeted, or should I say unwelcomed, by a hostile wife. I could see the disdain growing for me on a daily basis. Any attempt to bring a conversation that was centered around God, or my new life, was still met by the most severe resistance. I knew that one day a new marriage to Danielle was going to be birthed. I also knew that unfortunately, somehow, this present marriage was going to die first. I still tried to convince my wife of the reality of God, while I still had access to her ears, although it seemed hopeless. That night I lay in bed pondering the fate of my children. I was obviously aware of the reality that life with my three precious little ones would be affected deeply when this all came to pass. I had always told myself that I never wanted to wound my child the way I had been wounded. Parental abandonment was a burden I never wanted to place on my children. That night I cried processing all this. I cried as I talked to my God about not wanting my children to hurt. I pleaded with Him to keep their little hearts safe in His hands, as He had mine. I could feel the peace only He can offer sweep over me that night, allowing me to sleep. There is so much I can say about how this all ultimately unfolded. The truth is I was immature and young in this new life. I am sure that I made many mistakes and went about things the wrong way, as much as I did the right way. I just knew that I wanted to obey my Father at any cost.

My marriage systematically decayed, her hostility towards me growing daily. She forcefully told me to stop all this "God stuff" and to go back to being normal. She also told me that I needed to see a counselor, or someone for my mental health issues with this new life I was trying to live with God. I watched my children, especially my oldest one, my daughter, watch as all this unfolded. I knew she loved me with everything in her, and I her. I wanted that child to know she was a precious jewel to me. If I was going to eventually be limited in my time with her as a child, then I wanted her to take as much of my love with her as was possible. We would spend evenings and early mornings singing worship music, songs to Jesus, together. I would cry deeply as I heard the little voice of my daughter say the name of my great Savior. I pleaded with Him to save my children, and to keep them as His until the end.

As my robotic and estranged marriage was on its last breath, I knew it was almost time to lay it to rest. I sought the counsel of the two women who were mentoring me as to what I should do. Their counsel was that I was not allowed, ever, to divorce my wife, telling me that even if we ever got divorced that God would not allow me to marry Danielle. They reasoned that she was an unbeliever, and that God would never allow such a union. I was so confused! God had clearly spoken to me time and time again that Danielle was my wife-to-be. I knew this as clearly as anything He had ever spoken to me. I was chastened and rebuked by these women, they told me that I was probably severely angering God by even thinking of such things.

I went home one night in absolute fear and despair. I was so torn between what these two ladies were telling me, and what I was hearing from

God for myself. What a place to be. What a weight to carry. I really had fallen in love with Danielle as we spent more and more time together. I could see her softening towards me each time. The sad thing is I did not notice any such softening towards God on her part. I was so overwhelmed by the emotions of all these events occurring that I got real with God and told Him I was going to obey Him at any cost.

That night as I entered my home I walked directly into my bedroom. My wife was lying on the bed watching television. I grabbed her hand without saying a word to her and kneeled. I was kneeling before my God, even though she could not understand why I was kneeling, I did. I was humbling myself before my King, yet again seeking direction from Him. I began to erupt in tongues. My wife had never seen me do this, as I had hidden it from her. She already had enough reason to think I was crazy. I did not think her knowing I spoke in tongues would help her get any closer to accepting me or God. She stared silently at me as I cried and bellowed out to my God in a language neither of us could understand. Inside myself I pleaded with God to save my wife. I told Him that at any cost I would obey Him. If His will was for me to stay in this marriage, then I would. I would let go of my heart's desire for Danielle, even though I absolutely believed that He was the one that helped birth that desire in me. I was a broken man before my Father, as lost as I ever had been as a believer. I just wanted clear direction so that I could obey and move on.

After many tears and unknown words, I again was enveloped in peace. I let go of my wife's hands and went to sleep on the floor in the living room. This had been my resting place now for months. I heard the soft voice of my God telling me not to worry, that He would save her. I went to sleep that night hoping that the soon arriving tomorrow would bring clarity to me. I did not know where I was to go from here, but I knew that God would be faithful to show me the way.

I awoke that morning hoping to see a radically transformed wife. I entered that bedroom in the early morning hours expecting some radical improvement. To my dismay, my wife's hostility was at an all-time high. I could see her disgust with me. I quickly dressed for work, full of new emotional wounds. I remember the crisp cold air hitting my face, especially the areas where recent tears were falling.

I entered my car at about 7:45 am. I sat there in my driveway, and broke down before God. I cried and pleaded with Him to help me. I told Him I would obey whatever He wanted, but to please speak clearly to me about all this. A fifteen minute exchange between this broken man and his Father would result in the speaking of the soft voice inside me again. Although tears, cries, and loud worship music were all filling the car, I had no problem hearing His words to me. I was directed to call a previous patient of mine, a woman that I had treated many years prior. I did not understand. God's answer to my dilemma regarding Danielle and my wife was to call a woman that I barely knew at 8 am on a Tuesday morning and to ask her to meet me. The office was scheduled to open at 9 am. My office manager was always there early preparing for another day of business. I quickly obeyed and called her cell phone. She was alarmed that something was wrong that I would call her so early. I asked her to pull the patient's file from the back, to get her phone number, and to call her and ask her to meet with me. She immediately resisted this request. She abruptly asked me why, and stated that she would do no such thing unless I told her everything. Again, I voiced my request with no intention on disclosing why to her. Daily interventions to try and convince me I was crazy were already zealously underway; I did not think they needed any more fuel on their fire. After another refusal to comply I became more aggressive with her, resulting in her reluctantly agreeing to call the patient. She asked me again to tell her why I wanted this meeting, to which I hung up the phone immediately after telling her again to just to make the call.

I was so desperate to see what this next phone call would bring about. I was also so tired of being verbally attacked by the people in my life. I began to pray again in tongues knowing that my Father was at work in my life and in my present circumstances. Not even five minutes had passed before my manager called me back. She was surprised and confused as she relayed the results of the unexpected early call: the woman had agreed to meet me in 30 minutes at a local coffee shop. She then demanded me to tell her what was going on. I thanked her for making the call and hung up, telling her I might be late for work.

I did not know what to expect next. I was headed to a meeting with a woman I barely knew and, even crazier, I had no idea why. What a 20 minute drive to the coffee shop that was. I was so anxious and nervous, but at the same time excitement flooded my veins. Whatever was awaiting me was set in motion by God, my God! I walked into the coffee shop at about 8:20 am, with ten minutes to spare. I sought out an open table as there were not many. The location was extremely busy that early morning. The smell of fresh brewing coffee tried to interject its way into my thoughts, but they were quite resolved to only focus on the dilemma my heart was experiencing. I sat there in apparent silence, apparent because under my breath I was speaking in tongues in a subtle whisper. I had laid my Bible on the table before me. I knew that in less than ten minutes I would probably have my Father's answers to all I needed answered. I also knew that whatever would follow, would have to be obeyed by me. I was scared but still knew it was all going to be okay, because my Father was the one guiding my steps.

At precisely 8:30, in came the woman. I did not see her enter at first, I felt her enter. My "spider sense" went crazy. This time though, it did not feel bad, but extremely good. I could feel something all around her as if upon her. She was enveloped in a bright glow that natural eyes could not see. But my eyes now were far more than natural eyes. I watched her make her way to the table. I wondered if she even remembered me or what I looked like. Both of those questions were answered quickly as she walked straight to me. I was amazed that as she walked through the crowd that she was unnoticed by any of them. She carried such a presence of God with her, how could people around her be unaffected? Nonetheless, there she was not even three feet from me.

Her first words were not the typical "hello", or "what can I do for you?" No, her initial words were: "let us pray!" She then grabbed my hands and began to pray with a resolve and confidence that was amazing. I could see the people around us watching all this unfold. I felt kind of like a zoo animal in a crowd. But to tell the truth, I was so desperate for an answer from God that I really did not care about being embarrassed in order to get it. As a matter of fact, I had become more and more accustomed to God putting me in very uncomfortable circumstances and situations while asking me to do and say things that would make many run away. So in reality, this moment was quite normal for me now.

I remember with absolute clarity the prayer she prayed that great morning. I was so excited that she invoked my Father before she spoke a single word to me that morning. Praying put me at immediate ease. Her powerful voice began to speak as I felt her clench my hands a little tighter than before:

"Father, I thank you for sending me as a special messenger to your son."

What an opening! "Father", she knew Him as Father, too. She also stated that she was sent to His "son", me! I began to cry. He was faithful again. Layering another coat of love and acceptance around my heart with the very words He had her pray. I was so overwhelmed by the fact that God would send a personal messenger to me. His favor and kindness to me broke me down. As I sit here right now typing these very words I find myself wiping away the tears brought on by so many memories of His goodness to me. She stated that she was a "special" messenger. I didn't know if I had ever had a "special" one before. Surely, He had already sent many messengers before, but today I received my first special one. I knew that God had sent her. I also knew that because He had commissioned her to me I did not have to inquire for answers, because my Father already knew what I needed to hear.

She grabbed my Bible and opened to the Gospel of Mathew reading where Jesus said that if there was marital infidelity a man was allowed to divorce his wife and go in peace. She then took my hand and said:
"The Lord says His Word has set you free, go, and His grace will go with you."

What could I ever say to all that but just break down crying. My loving Father was there for me again--real answers for me again. He cared so much for me, and all the struggles that I went through; He still does. He was never a God far off to me, but right there, always listening, and always ready to step right in to guide and rescue His son. I left the coffee shop now resolved and free.

Chapter 18: More Demonic Manifestations and Holy Fire

A few months later my broken marriage filled with infidelity was dissolved, and I was again a single man, but not for long. The day after my divorce was finalized, I found myself hospitalized for an emergency gallbladder removal. What a life I live! Danielle was with me at my side in the hospital. We were notified of the news of the divorce finally being official. I looked into my wife-to-be's eyes and expressed my sincere and deep love for her, and told her that I did not want to spend another day without her as my bride. I felt led by the Holy Spirit to find a way to make our union complete in the sight of God. I found a bed and breakfast in Ohio that also married people on the property. Me and my soon to be, now Spirit-filled and Christian, bride agreed to drive there the next day and be single no more. Danielle was now a Holy Spirit-filled baby Christian that loved God, my God, Jesus! Let me catch you up on how exactly that took place.

After my encounter with the woman at the coffee shop I initiated divorce proceedings. My wife had already wanted me gone long before, and as a result she hired an attorney that brought accusations of my insanity and potential instability due to my new radical Christian faith. This attorney began to build a case painting a picture that I was a threat to the safety of her and my children. My attorney advised me to stay in the house as long as I could so that she would not be able to claim abandonment, so I did. But this situation did not work out well; the level of hostility from her was something I did not want my children to be exposed to, so I left. I had nowhere to live, so Danielle took me in.

Again, controversial events are about to be shared with you. I was now about five months old in the Lord. I knew that Danielle was now one day going to be my wife, although I did not know how all this would take place. I found myself staying at her small apartment just off campus to the college where she was working towards a physical therapy degree. She was absolutely unwilling at that time to even hear the whispered name of Jesus without pulling an all-out temper tantrum. This was such an uncomfortable situation for me, but there I was right in the middle of it all due to circumstance. We spent every day together, and every night too. Yes, I fell into sexual immorality with this precious promised woman of mine. Each time I would try to justify it because I knew she was going to be my wife one day, but deep down I knew God did not feel the same. After each sexual encounter I would quietly leave her apartment, and go into my car pretending to need to go somewhere. Once in my car I would cry contrite tears before my God. Sometimes this would last for hours. After a period of time I would eventually go back into the apartment resolved to not fall again into the sexual trap, only to fail time and time again. I felt so ashamed that I would continue to do the very things I knew I was not supposed to do. I tried to spend more time in churches to see if that would help me overcome this struggle, but to no avail.

I was so afraid that I had screwed up the whole thing, and I was not sure if God was still going to let me have Danielle as my bride. I was terrified. This behavior went on for close to 2 months. I was so desperate for Danielle to get saved. I prayed day after day pleading with my Father to please bring her home to His Kingdom. I remember asking the two pastor ladies to pray, too. Their response was a dagger to my heart. They told me that if God did save her, then He would probably not let her marry me. I was devastated. I walked away from that conversation to sit alone and ponder that possibility. I talked to God about it and told Him that I would so much rather she get to know Him and be saved, even if it meant she would not be allowed to marry me afterwards. I cried at the thought of this. Still my desire for this woman I was madly in love with was to see her saved. Finally the monumental day came to pass.

It was just another Saturday morning at the onset. I awoke next to Danielle, as we both laid there and talked about the plans for our day. Danielle had a very peculiar alarm clock on the night stand by her bed; it was a famous cartoon character, that instead of a typical alarm, it repeated well-known humorous one-liners. I was quite accustomed to it by this time. As we laid there continuing to talk in those early morning hours, suddenly the alarm clock began to sound off louder than I had ever heard it. But, this time there was no quirky cartoon voice. The sounds coming out from that device were horrifying. It sounded like an auditory collage of piercing screams. In the background behind these screams you could hear multiple prevalent voices speaking in an unknown language that could be described in no other way than demonic. Along with all this, the sounds of clashing metals also seemed to permeate from this device. I could barely bear to listen to those nightmarish sounds, and I looked over to see if Danielle heard them as well. Her response was rapid. She reached over me to turn the clock off; she stated that maybe it needed new batteries.

I could not believe this event had really gone unnoticed by Danielle. So many past supernatural events had already taken place in her apartment while I had been there. Each time for some reason she was not able to see or hear the events. To say, I was frustrated by this would be so insufficient. I pleaded with God to let her see with her eyes the spiritual manifestations occurring in her apartment, in hope that it would lead her to salvation. This morning I thought for an instant that God had granted my request. But, by her response to the ghastly noises, it appeared as if this experience was mine, and mine alone, to witness. Shortly thereafter I got ready for work, and left giving her a soft kiss and a heart-felt "I love you."

I drove to work that morning praying again for the salvation of my precious Danielle. The three-hour shift passed by very quickly that day. I kept replaying the horrible voices I had heard that morning. I just could not understand why God allowed me to hear it and not her. After all, I was already aware of the reality of demons. I had already had over a hundred personal experiences in the past four to five months. Later in this book I will share some of the more shocking ones with you. I packed up to leave the office and called Danielle letting her know to meet me at a restaurant near her place for lunch. The long 35-minute drive gave me some more time to pray for her. I was not sure how much prayer it was going to take, but I was not going to stop until she was saved. As I arrived at the restaurant she was already seated in the back in a booth. I greeted her with another kiss and a loving hug. I prepared to have another conversation in which I was not allowed to talk about God. It was in that exact moment that an explosion of hope erupted before my eyes. Danielle with a loud and excitable voice bellowed out:

"Those were demons this morning speaking through the alarm clock, weren't they?!"

My eyes lit up with joy! She had finally heard something too!

"YES!" I answered. "You heard it, too?!"

A state of panic seemed to grip her as she responded:

"Those sounds were horrifying. Why did it happen?"

The following hours were spent sharing the reality of such entities as demons and fallen angels. She listened attentively to my stories and my testimonies. I had a captive and curious audience: she was finally willing to listen. After a detailed description of the operation of the demonic realm, at least to the level of my understanding back then, I changed the topic: I finally began to tell her about Jesus. After all, if the demons were real, that also meant that God was real too. This seemed to register with her, and she began to process the last 26 years of her life in the face of these recently obtained truths. That whole night was spent talking about spiritual things with Danielle; I was so happy. That night we went to bed spiritually closer than we ever had been up to that point. I was finally allowed to say Jesus' name in her presence without being cussed out, or having something thrown at me. This was the long awaited and prayed for progress. I would love to say that this led to her immediate salvation, but that was not exactly what took place. We spent the next three days talking and reading about spiritual things from the Bible. It wasn't until the following Tuesday morning that Danielle accepted salvation.

She had accompanied me to a counseling session with a Christian counselor I had already been seeing for a few months. I had begun to see this counselor as a result of my attorney wanting me to show I was in counseling for my marital problems, an appeasement of my soon to be ex-wife's attorney's requests. Truth be told, most of the sessions were spent with me discovering the new creation I had become in Jesus. On that Tuesday morning session, Danielle accompanied me into my counselor's office. There I introduced him to the woman I had been talking to him about for a while now. We shared the occurrence with the alarm clock. He was excited too, but not as much as I was. He then shared the simple message of the cross with Danielle, in a way that touched her deeply. It was right then and there that she accepted Jesus and his grace unto Salvation, and became born again.

It was so awesome she was a believer now! We could finally become equally yoked, and I could now marry her after my divorce was final. What a glorious day! We spent the next 4 days talking and learning about God together, sunrise to sundown. We were two peas in a pod. I barely went to work that whole time; all I wanted to do was be with her and God.

The ensuing Sunday morning would eventually come, and I asked her to come to the large church where I had spoken in tongues the first time, and she agreed. We woke up early in order to make the first service at 7 am. We arrived punctually at the church, and were greeted by loving and smiling faces. We took our seats, and the worship began. I could see Danielle being touched by the beautiful melodies sang to the King we now had in common. It was a dream come true to stand there and hold the hand of the woman I loved, while giving praise and thanksgiving together to our God. The teaching would then follow--another service on the coming end day tribulation. It seemed everywhere I went that this was the topic of interest in the first few months of my salvation. The message would eventually conclude, and the alter call to receive the Holy Spirit began. Danielle decided to go, and I went with her, to support her.

We were escorted with others into a separate room, where they would pray for those who came forward to receive the Holy Spirit and wanted to speak in tongues. She asked God for both and began to try and speak in tongues. The following events were wild. Danielle began to release piercing sounds; sounds I have never heard a human make, nor do I think it is even possible for anyone to replicate such sounds in the natural. It sounded like a screeching lamb. The sounds then became louder, and she began to shake. A bunch of the pastors came running to her, and they all laid their hands on her, beginning to intercede for her. I raised my hands to God and began speaking in tongues myself, excited and overwhelmed by the event.

Before I go on, I have to give you some history on an event that had happened to me months prior, so that you can fully understand. I was still in the Baptist church back then. I was attending a weekly Wednesday evening service, and we were about to take communion. This was the first time I had ever done that in a corporate setting. They had handed out the wafers and the tiny containers of grape juice. I held one in each hand as I sat there with my eyes closed and my mind and heart focused on God. It was such a privilege for me to share in the holy act of Communion. The pastor started to pray. Before taking part in the Communion, I thanked God with all my heart for having mercy on me. As I sat there, I heard Him say some very personal things to me, after which a radical experience unfolded.

I felt a wave of tangible fire sweep over me from my head to my toes. I was alarmed and startled beyond measure. I quickly opened my eyes in a panic to see if I was actually burning. To my surprise there was nothing notable to the natural eyes. I began to cry out in a frenzied whisper:
"God what are you doing to me?!"

Funny thing was I knew it was Him doing whatever this whole thing was. I had never felt anything like this before. I had no idea how to respond to such a thing. I felt his comforting voice answer me, and tell me to stand up.

"God, are you serious? You want me to stand up now, in front of all these people?"

His answer followed quickly:

"Yes, trust me."

My body began to shake uncontrollably, as I felt like I was being consumed by this unseen blaze around me. I took a deep breath, and stood up. The fire intensified, and all of a sudden my jaw began to shake violently. I grabbed my jaw with both hands and pushed it upwards to keep my mouth closed.

"God, I am scared."

"Trust me and open your mouth."

I could feel His love and patience as He was teaching new things to His young son, a very startled and scared young son, but still a very willing one.

"God, are you about to make me do the tongues thing?" I innocently asked.

At that point in time I had never spoken in tongues, and had only heard about it vaguely. His response again was the same:

"Trust me, and open your mouth."

I did trust Him, and now I was about to prove it. I released the hold on my jaw, and relaxed my facial muscles. My hand lifted to Him, and I yielded to His will.

In that moment words came forth from deep within me that were so eloquent and precious, it was obvious they did not originate from me. After about two minutes of the most awesome prayer I had ever heard coming out of my mouth I dropped like a sack of potatoes. I was emptied of any natural strength. I had no idea what had just happened, but it was God doing it. Multiple people came by me and lifted me back up, encouraging me that the Holy Spirit had just spoken through me! I did not know what to say, so I just smiled and stated that it was not I saying those great things. Let us now fast forward back to Danielle.

As we were walking to the room to pray for Danielle to receive the Holy Spirit, I felt that same fire come down on her. I rapidly went to say something to her, but the Holy Spirit told me not to. So in mid-sentence I stopped and looked at her smiling, saying that great things were about to happen to her. I could feel the great supernatural heat on my hand, the one that was holding hers.

There we were--Danielle emitting sounds that were coming from her innermost being, while a multitude of ministers laid hands on her, all erupting in tongues. What a sight! It was then that a piercingly loud sound erupted from my wife-to-be, and she collapsed. The ministers quickly got her softly to a seated position on a chair, and continued to fervently pray in tongues over her. I approached her, and hugged her, as the ministers began to pray over both of us now. They did not know us at all, yet the setting was incredibly intimate. After a little while longer of praying, they stopped and got both of our attention. By now Danielle was again lucid, but still blown away from the event. It was then that the head minister there began to speak:

"You two are highly anointed of the Lord."

I did not exactly know what that meant, but I felt like it was a great thing!

He then began to speak again:

"Enjoy your ministry."

Now I was ecstatic! He had said the word "your," that meant there would be an us, Danielle and me. God had decided to allow me to still marry that great woman I was so in love with, despite all of my mistakes. What an unforgettable day!

We eventually exited the room to shouts of joy from the ministers that had been part of that whole supernatural process. With big smiles on our faces we headed out of the building to our car. We were so shocked by the whole thing neither of us were really speaking just yet. As we walked to the car in the large parking lot I felt God directed me to take Danielle back in there for the next service, the 10 am. I did not know why He wanted this, but it did not matter: I just obeyed. We again walked in, and were escorted to two open seats. Again the worship music began. I stood and raised my hands to God in thanksgiving. I turned to Danielle expecting to see the same. Instead, my soon to be wife was curled up on the floor in a ball violently weeping. I did not know what to do, but I was not alarmed because God was there with us. Whatever was happening to Danielle was a good thing. Some of the ushers came by to offer her tissues, but she just kept weeping. They all looked at me and smiled, I returned their smiles silently. We all knew that God was doing something great with His new daughter, and that it was going to be okay.

At the end of the worship, Danielle stood up and wiped away the abundance of tears on her face with the tissues the ushers had left for her and spoke:

"I think it is okay for us to go now."

I never really asked her exactly what God did with her there on the floor that day. I knew that it was personal and precious to her, just like so many things God had already done with me. We embraced each other and walked to the car together to leave for real this time. What a great beginning to our new lives, full of great promises and hope, and now even a "ministry."

The following morning I awoke along-side of Danielle--the new Danielle. I rapidly recalled all of the events from the previous day. I was quick to make sure it was not all a hopeful dream. I softly nudged her to wake her up. I wanted so badly to talk to her. She opened her groggy eyes and smiled. We exchanged a simple and precious kiss, and exchanged the most genuine I love you we ever had. We both lay there, and replayed the great things that had happened not even 24 hours earlier. We both thanked God and got out of bed. Danielle headed for the shower, I headed to her kitchen. I sat there and drank a glass of water at the small kitchen table. I began to pray in tongues while I smiled the whole time. I was so excited to see what was going to happen now, now that I had a Spirit-filled companion that was obviously also called by God for some really cool purpose. We felt so blessed. About ten minutes later the water in the shower turned off, and shortly after the bathroom door opened. There she stood, the born-again Danielle. She looked at me and gestured with her index finger in my direction as she prepared to make a very important statement:

"Let's get something straight right now: From now on you are #2... And no more sex until we are married!"

Wow! What a statement. You would expect my response to be anything other than the one I actually gave. With a large sense of relief I cried out:

"Halleluiah! Thank you God!"

I was so happy that I would now have her support to overcome the struggle of sexual temptations with her. The fact that God had now taken the spot of #1 in her life only made me happier. I was not jealous of Him being so important to her; after all he was # 1 to me, too. I was so happy to have a spiritual partner by my side. My walk with God was so wonderful. I am sure that in some ways it resembled the relationship He had way back in the beginning with Adam; the incredible intimacy they must have shared alone in the Garden of Eden, just the two of them. No distractions to dissuade Adam from developing a completely transparent and trusting relationship with his Creator and best friend. Learning about the very creation he was living in from the One that made it. No pressure of performance, or impossible imposed expectations to achieve. No competition with any peers. No open door for feelings of inadequacy, and failure from his past mistakes to shame him from looking with confidence into the eyes of his God. What a wonderful beginning to this relationship. And with all this, a loving and all-knowing God looked down and saw that man alone was not a good thing. Danielle may not have been formed from one of my extracted ribs, but it felt like she was a template that perfectly fit together with me, completing the created man that God had in mind when he breathed His breath into the dust destined to become me. She was the missing link to my very existence in this realm. I knew this with all my heart. Not because I needed her, but because God created me to need her. We were created to be one, not two separate people that decided to unite. I can't really tell you how I've always known this, but I have. Without her I know I would not have been able to become the man or minister I am today. I am so grateful for this wonderful woman, wife, and friend.

Chapter 19: He Disciplines Those He Loves

It is here that I will now share one of my greatest moments of stupidity in my Christian walk. These next events were so intricate and foundational in forming my new character. After Danielle was born again we started to talk about our plans to marry. We had to wait until the divorce process of my current marriage was finalized, which was still a few months away. We knew for sure that both of us were called by God to unite, and we both really loved each other, and wanted to be married. Without other feasible temporary living options, living together prior to marriage brought about special challenges. We had already crossed over boundaries and lines that single Christians are not supposed to cross. So here we were: two baby believers, our new found God, and this dark world surrounding us. We wanted to live the life God wanted us to, obedient to His will. The sexual temptations that attacked us, especially me, were overwhelming. As an immature and selfish man, I reasoned that because she was one day going to be my wife anyways, that it would be okay if we fooled around from time to time. I had no idea how dangerous what I was doing was. Let me go on to tell you how my all seeing and loving Father decided to teach me one of the most important lessons He ever has.

We had been living together for close to two months by this time. My divorce proceedings were coming along, but not fast enough for me. My Christian walk was laced with supernatural manifestations of every sort. Almost everything seemed perfect. Inside the pit of my stomach though, I knew something was wrong. This sensation of unrest would ignite every time I engaged into sexual interactions of any sort with Danielle. I knew that it was not right, but over and over I kept finding myself giving into this struggle. A fueling fire that prompted me to keep seeking this form of acceptance from my future wife was a vast trail of rejection and insecurities left behind from my previous life. Physical affection from Danielle made me feel loved by her. Anytime I felt insecure in our relationship, I would immediately seek comfort from her through physical means. The tug of war on my emotions and my spiritual well-being was wearing this man down. I knew, but pretended not to know, that God was not okay with my behavior. Then one day it was made evident that my King was not willing to allow me to pretend any more.

It was in the middle of a work week at the office. It was a typical mid-week morning. The office was full of patients and staff. I was my usual zealous self, running around the office preaching about the newest things I had learned about my God while occasionally performing the duties of a doctor. I found myself walking through one of the large adjusting rooms when unexpectedly, a newer patient of mine arose off of the adjusting table, and approached me. She silently looked me straight in the eyes. I barely knew this woman, but the little I had discerned about her told me that she walked with God, too. I could feel a seriousness come over the exchange that was about to take place between the two of us. I knew whatever was about to take place was God directed. I braced myself emotionally, as she began to speak: "The Lord says that you are off the path! And that you better return to it soon!"

I wanted to pee my pants right there. I knew she was another messenger from God sent into my path to help me. My pride did not allow me to show in that moment the true internal impact those words had. I offered a fake smile and a slight nod of the head to acknowledge hearing what she had said, and then I walked out of the room. I reflected in silence my position now before my God. I was so scared! I did not know what to do. I had always run from any relationship in the past once I felt rejected by the other person. I now knew I had angered my God, my best friend, my King. I felt like I now was stained by my mistakes and that His displeasure with me would take away the precious relationship we had experienced up to that point. The smart thing would have been to repent and cease all ungodly behavior and to turn back to the path. I did not have the grasp of the greatness of His grace available to His children that I know now. I was still very much programmed from decades of performance based acceptance. And unfortunately, some of that faulty programming interfered with my relationship with Him. I withdrew in shame. This only made me feel more insecure and rejected from the One whose opinion meant everything to me. I never felt as ashamed as I did that day. I felt like I had just thrown away the greatest thing I ever was given: my wonderful relationship with God. The result of this wrong kind of thinking pushed me further into the hole of sexual sin with Danielle. I grabbed hold of the perceived acceptance I felt from physical closeness from her to try and find whatever comfort I could to deal with the shame suffocating me. This went on for a few days, and then one of the wildest days in my walk took place:

I had been pondering the words that woman had spoken to me days before in my office. I felt like I finally was at a place to really talk to God about it. I already knew my behavior was all wrong, but I still wanted to try and salvage whatever part of my relationship with Him that I could. I was driving to work that day and I began to pray. I remember word for word that simple prayer that would change me forever:

"God...if I am living in rebellion that would send me to Hell, please give me a sign in my face that I can't ignore, in Jesus' name."

The prayer ended as I pulled into the parking lot of my office. What happened next was insane. I walked right into my office, almost as if guided by an external force. One of my assistants saw me and greeted me. I was so caught up in the spiritual moment that I was unable to respond. As I entered my office I approached a stack of teaching DVDs I had accumulated over the past months, most of which I had not watched yet. Some of them were from services I had attended where I really liked the message and purchased a copy of it on my way out. It was one of these DVDs that I grabbed. I had no idea why I was doing this. I recall the look on my assistant's face as she watched me. She had followed me into my office because she had some business related questions. But my lack of acknowledging her presence or her initial greeting gave her pause to not ask anything just yet. In a very mechanical type of movement I took the DVD out of its case and slowly inserted it into a DVD player in the entertainment hutch. As the device loaded the inserted disc's contents I stood silently staring at the TV screen.

To this very day I still do not really recall the thoughts roaming through my head in the minutes I just described. I don't think I even realized what I was doing. I knew that my medical assistant was in the room with me, but it was an almost unconscious awareness. Eventually the disc would begin to play. As it did my peculiar behavior continued to unfold.

I grabbed the remote control and fast forwarded the disc to one hour and seven minutes. I would love to tell you that I had a reason why, but at that time I did not. I had never watched this DVD before. The disc was a recording of a service I had attended almost two months prior, at the large church where my wife received the Holy Spirit. It was part of a six disc series with teachings on the coming tribulation. I had bought them and immediately stored them on an upper shelf in my office. I did not know how important that disc would end up being for me one day. Before I continue, I want to remind you of the precise prayer I had prayed mere minutes prior:

"God if I am living in rebellion that would send me to Hell, please give me a sign in my face that I can't possibly deny, in Jesus' name."

Well, as the DVD began to play at the one hour and seven minute mark, my immediate answer would come. The cameras were relaying the imagery of the head pastor speaking to the congregation. There was a subtle two to three-second pause before he began. He seemed to be quite serious with his facial appearance. Then he began to speak:

"Hell was never made for man, it was made for Satan and a third of the angels that went with him and rebelled against God. But, if you are going to follow Satan, and you are going to live like the devil, even though it was not intended for you, you are going to get exactly as he is going to get."

As if that was not enough the response got even more personal: the camera at that exact moment panned into the crowd and stopped on a very bewildered face in the crowd: mine! My face took up the entire screen as the pastor's voice again began to bellow in the background:

"I don't know how to make it plainer than that! But God's man obeyed HIM! It said about Noah numerous times: thus did Noah continually as God said!"

I hit STOP on the remote and turned off the TV. I looked at my assistant and quickly left the room without ever hearing the questions that she wanted to ask me. I got in my car shortly thereafter and left the office. I rapidly drove to our apartment and grabbed the few suitcases of my personal belongings that had followed me to Danielle's apartment. Very shortly thereafter I was signing a rental sheet at a local motel. As I entered the room I placed my things on the floor and on the bed I was sitting on.

I replayed the message over and over in my mind. There was no way I could possibly write it off as a coincidence. I was scared beyond my worst nightmares. God, my Father, had spoken very clearly to me in that message. He said that if I did not stop, I was going to Hell with Satan. Can you even imagine how I felt? I did not know how to make things right between me and my Father again, but I was resolved to do whatever it took. I eventually called Danielle from the hotel room and relayed to her what had happened. I apologized to her for allowing us to fall into repeated sexual immorality, with me usually being the initiator. I told her I could no longer live with her unmarried to me, and that I had to make things right with God. I really do not remember her immediate reaction; I was way too concerned about how my God felt. I spent most of that night alone in the hotel room, in silence trying to figure out how to make up for what I had done. I wanted God, and I wanted to go back to how we were before I started acting like an idiot. I received no answer yet at that time as to what I was supposed to do.

The night went on and on exactly like that until about 3 am. I found myself looking at the ceiling tiles when all of a sudden I felt something paralyze me and pin me to the bed. I could not see anything with my natural eyes, but that did not change the fact it was really happening to me. I was terrified! I tried desperately to get my body to respond and move, but to no avail. I then in even more desperation tried to call out for help to either natural ears or God's. But, my mouth was paralyzed as well! I could not move or speak. My heart and mind were caught in a frenzy of panic and fear. This went on for several minutes. Even though I could not move or speak at least nothing worse was happening to me. It was then as I started to lose all hope of a good outcome to all this, that God stepped in.

The soft whispering voice inside me had not spoken to me all day, that is, until now.

"Son, when you are in rebellion, you are not under my protection."

I was in rebellion! Right then and there, I was in rebellion to the living God, my Father, Jesus, The Holy Spirit! How had I gotten to this place?!

What was going to happen next?

I now knew I was under attack from the demonic realm. I had just heard God tell me that I was not under His protection. Did this mean that He was about to let them kill me? I knew the demons hated me with everything they had. I was preparing myself for a very horrifying fate. Then it dawned on me:

"I can't speak with my mouth, but I can talk to God in my thoughts!"

Without wasting another minute I cried out from a place of the deepest fear I had ever experienced!

"God, I am sooooo soooooo sorry for what I have done, and for rebelling against you! I will not do it again, please forgive me! Please!"

I could feel tears running down my face. My muscles were not working but my tear glands sure were. All of a sudden I could talk again, but I still could not move. I began to scream Jesus' name as loud as I could! "Jesus, help me!"

Over and over I bellowed that out of my mouth. It was shortly after that I could again move. As I realized my body was mine again to command, I lunged off the bed and ran out of the room in my underwear. I ran half way across the large parking lot in the dead of night as I tried to escape the demon attacking and find safety. Then I thought: Why did I think that I would be safer outside than in my room? Surely the demon could follow me outside just as easily. I dropped to my knees right there under the half moon and the stars, and pleaded with my Father to restore me to His house and His favor. Even more than that, I begged for His protection to once again cover my life. I cried like a baby, and told Him again that I was so sorry for how I had acted with Danielle, His daughter.

I knew I was forgiven in that very instant, and returned to His good graces. I cried tears of gratitude and slowly raised my grateful hands as if reaching out to Him in Heaven to say thank you, Father. Again, my Father had been faithful and loving to me. The next day I met with Danielle and laid down the foundation of our future. There would be no more physical contact until we were married; I would not be alone with her in a house: I always brought a chaperone to sit between us, with no exceptions! My over the top reaction puzzled Danielle, but then again, she had not been subjected to the chastisement by the hand of God that I had just had. My new behavior was not meant to please her, but my God.

Fast forward: I am in the hospital in the middle of May. My gallbladder, latent with gallstones, had probably just been discarded after its removal from within me. Danielle was at my side when I woke up from my surgery, holding my hand with a chaperone in the recovery room. I looked at her and told her I loved her, and that I wanted to marry her ASAP!

Chapter 20: Modern Day Idols

We had just found out the day before the surgery that my divorce was final. She looked at me and responded to my request made under partial anesthetic with a sincere smile and two teary eyes. Forty eight hours later I was released from the hospital, with a set of temporary crutches, and one less gallbladder. We went home, packed, and headed to a beautiful facility in Ohio on a lake, along with our two friends. Their company was necessary not only as chaperones but also as witnesses to our wedding. As we arrived at our destination in Ohio, we settled in and prepared to be married the next afternoon. That evening we all sat by the natural wood burning fireplace and fellowshipped with the owner of the facility. He was the one that was going to marry us the next day. We shared that we were recent born again Christians and told him a little about our recent lives. He smiled and got up quickly to go get something.

Danielle and I looked at each other not knowing what our sharing had just brought about, but, oh well; it was too late now to take it back. A few minutes later, the nice man returned with a picture book and some newspaper clippings. He went on to tell us the story of how he was also a small aircraft pilot, and years ago he had flown missionaries into Africa and South America. On one of these trips, the men entered into a tribe of cannibals and tried to preach the gospel to them. Sadly, they were killed by the tribe and their bodies eaten. Later, the missionaries' wives also travelled to the same tribe and miraculously the tribe members received Jesus and salvation. Another miracle was that the widows showed a tremendous act of mercy by forgiving them for their husband's deaths. He went on to tell us they had made a movie based on the true story called The Edge of the Spear. A movie we now own. Coincidence? I think not.

We went to bed in separate rooms that night knowing it would be the last night we would ever have to. I was so nervous for the wedding to come. I was not just getting married for the first time as a new creation, but I was marrying God's daughter.

Amazingly, I slept like a baby. The next morning was perfect. Sunny sky, warm weather, and the perfect bride! God was about to give His precious daughter's hand to me in marriage. I took this so seriously. I knew He really was protective over her, after all I knew how protective He had been about me. I knew that He would always be watching over her. Our vows were exchanged with smiles and tears, and there we were: a beautiful couple united in the presence of God. The verse: "What God brings together let no man bring asunder," had special meaning to me that day, more special than most can imagine. God had truly brought us together. He had gone to tremendous ends to help us see all this through. As much as Eve was created to be with Adam, Danielle was created to be with me--and me with her. We were so thankful to God for each other. We spent another day at the resort and then returned home secretly married.

Upon returning home things really became even crazier. One of the next mornings, God spoke very clearly to Danielle to quit school and to come work at the chiropractic office. Her radical obedience to our Father always encouraged me, and helped to grow my personal faith. She wrote all of her instructors and her classmates a profound letter. She stated in the letter that she had found Jesus, and that she was now going to live a life for Him, following His desires for her. She also stated that He told her to quit school and begin a ministry with her new husband, me, in his practice. Can you imagine how this letter must have gone over? Well let me tell you some of how it went.

Friends began aggressive intervention attempts to try and "rescue" her from me and God. Family members called the local police department associated with her college, stating that she had been kidnapped by me. We actually had to show up together at the police department, showing that she was okay, and that she had married me of her own free will and last, but not least, that she was safe. This erratic behavior by everyone in her life brought us to temporarily avoid all of them, until things calmed down. We thought that after they saw how happy she was, that they would also be happy for her, and stop the whole ridiculous assault on our marriage and our walk with God. Needless to say that is not what happened, and unfortunately there are still a lot of hard feelings about me and our new lifestyle.

About a month later Danielle felt that she had an open door to meet up with a friend and share her testimony and the Gospel. Let me lay a foundation for the spiritual back round of this meeting: This woman had given Danielle a tarot card reading about six months prior – a month or two before Danielle and I had begun dating, while we were acquaintances. This reading had real spiritual power; Danielle was not simply told vague newspaper horoscope type words of flattery and promises of adventure. My name and relationship to Danielle had specifically been brought up and as the medium, her friend, had felt a horrible fear and panic that I was a predator, she warned Danielle that she should probably stay away from me, especially as a romantic interest. Specifically, when I was brought up she had a vision of a black panther who would sexually assault Danielle. Clearly, whatever spirit was speaking at that reading definitely did not like me, and did not want me around Danielle.

Just the kind of person I wanted to have lunch with, right? Rhetorical question. I still decided to go, mostly for my wife. I wanted to do whatever I could for Danielle, and she felt strongly that I should meet with her and give her the gospel, knowing the destructiveness of the spirit guides that were tormenting her friend. I also must admit that I was quite interested in the opportunity to preach the gospel to someone so taken in by the dark side of the spiritual realm. We eventually met up at a casual Italian restaurant by our apartment. The casual exchange of simple handshakes brought us all to be seated at a small round table. The waitress had not even had a chance to introduce herself, when the conversation got heated and spiritual. Eventually the conversation centered on Danielle's new faith in Jesus. Understand, Danielle used to be caught up in all that stuff too; she had actively prayed to be a vampire, astroprojected, used hallucinogenic drugs, and was considering seeking shamanistic powers at the time that we met. This was all very confusing and shocking to her friend that now (only a few months since she had last seen her) Danielle was adamantly professing the reality of Jesus, the God of the Bible, and Him alone, as God. My wife and I tried to convince her friend as to the reality of Hell, and that Jesus was the only way to salvation through grace by faith.

As this heated exchange progressed Danielle's friend became severely agitated. She felt that we were judging choices that she was making with her life, looking down on her while we ourselves were still not fully conformed to the image of Christ in the Bible. I'm certain she was spiritually attacked to view us as hypocrites telling her that she was required to live by the standards of the Bible, while in her minds we were sinners that had done all these sinful things in our past. We were exasperated that we were simply telling her what God was telling us to tell her, that we weren't the ones setting the standards for salvation, we were just sharing the rules of the game! Our lunch appeared to end in frustration, but Danielle went to spend some time alone to talk to her friend one on one, in hopes that it would be more fruitful.

What happened next while they were alone became very strange. Danielle felt it was important to stress to her friend that the Bible was absolute truth, that the God of the Bible, Jesus, is the only God, and all other gods are demons, including whatever spirits her friend was channeling to do tarot cards readings and was leading her in making life decisions. Her friend pulled a small, wooden Buddha statue out of her coat pocket and explained its spiritual importance to her. Who says that Christianity is boring?! What are you supposed to do once the demon possessed Buddha statue comes out?! Danielle perceived that carrying this small idol in her pocket and being able to touch and hold it brought her friend comfort, which was strange and frightening to her in light of what Danielle herself had just learned about the reality of Hell and demonic powers.

And then came God to the rescue: Danielle heard the Holy Spirit tell her that he wanted to speak to her friend directly through the Bible, to tell her friend to open up a Bible to any page and that He would speak directly to her through the scriptures. Danielle pulled her Bible out of her bag and handed it to her to open to any page. God is faithful. The page she opened it to was Isaiah 44: Danielle began to read aloud starting in verse 9 through verse 20 about men making idols of wood and stone and worshipping them. Her friend was not convinced: she felt that the idols in her life were perhaps money or greed, but refused to believe that God was trying to tell her that the small wooden statue she possessed was indeed an idol. Danielle returned home somewhat sad, but amazed how clearly God wants to reach and communicate with each of us and His ability to do so.

That night, sleeping in our apartment, at approximately 2:05 am, Danielle and I were both abruptly awakened at the same time. We were quickly gathered to a state of awareness, an awareness that something else was in our bedroom other than us. We heard our cat hiss and run out of the room.

We could not see anything in the natural, but we had no doubt that we were not alone. Out of no-where we heard a loud sound, and a stackable dresser went flying across the room breaking into pieces, and spilling our clothes all over the floor. Now you would figure this would cause most people to run out of the apartment, but not us. Though we were young Christians, we were both already more than seasoned in spiritual warfare. We both had already had so many experiences where the demonic forces had risen up against us, but each time so did our Father! We were spiritual warriors in training, and to this day we still are. After hearing all this craziness, Danielle and I looked at each other for an instant and then began to battle back. We simultaneously commanded the demon out of our apartment in the authority Jesus gave us as His children. In an instant the room was cleared of unwanted visitors, following which we laid back down, and went back to sleep.

As we eventually awoke the next morning, we processed the event, trying to figure out why that demon had attacked us then, at 2:05 am Danielle felt that it was some sort of backlash from ministering to her friend, so she called her to make sure she was okay. She answered almost immediately and Danielle asked her how she was. Her friend shared that she was pretty sleepless the night before, that she had been thinking about what we had said, and that if we were that concerned about her, that if we really thought the spiritual things she was involved with were unsafe, that maybe she should consider our advice. Just after 2 am she woke up, threw away her tarot cards, and cancelled some New Age Religion classes she was registered with online. She went on to say that the conversation we had with her at lunch gave her pause, and that she had been reflecting on the possibility of the Jesus we preached being true. It made sense now why the demon would come and throw a temper tantrum in our bedroom. What a victory!

Chapter 21: The Laodicean Church

The next couple of days were spent trying to figure out what our new lives were supposed to look like. Danielle had started to come to my office, and began to teach herself the intricate workings of the business. Meanwhile, I continued to learn how to be a more proficient fisher of men, not to mention we both pondered the ministry to come. It was living a brand new life. It really is a wild ride to walk with God, I mean, really walk with God. The office staff was quite resistant to my wife. In lieu of how ineffective all their recent attempts were at dissuading my new protocols, they kept their opinions to themselves. Even with all this, their silent disdain was very evident.

Nevertheless, Danielle and I were there for Kingdom business. I was so disinterested in the daily functions of the office. The financial effects the new me had on the office were quite devastating but I really was unfazed. The world around me was still full of lost fish; this is all I could focus on. In reality, it is all I ever wanted to focus on. Having a personal understanding as to the reality of Hell was a tremendous motivating factor, especially when things became difficult. I did not want one person to end up in that horrifying place on my watch if it could have been avoided. Every time I was engaged in trying to dissuade someone from continuing in their path leading to damnation, I would always envision that person being the old me. It would bring chills over me, and eventually lead me back again to grateful tears towards my Savior. I will tell you that God was really an incredible co-pilot through all this. Every time we were sharing His reality with someone, He would always bring out the bells and whistles: prophetic words, healings, miracles, supernatural words of knowledge and wisdom and so much more. It was evident through my life that the awesome and interactive God of the Bible had not changed.

It was always so discouraging to me when I would get into conversations with other believers about my walk and my God, the One I had found in the basement of my house. The level of unbelief they would release into the conversation was as deadly as the exhaust of a car in a closed garage. Each time I could feel their doubt and unwillingness to believe that God was like the One I was walking with it felt like large abrasive waves hitting against the wall of faith I had guarding my heart. My God was alive! He was real! He was for me! The attempts to dissuade me from believing the radicalness of my God were useless. I was not going to let go of the great new life I had. I could not understand how they called themselves Christians. It was evident they did not believe that the God in the Bible still was in the business of being God--not to mention the absolute rejection of believing that Christians are supposed to be baptized in the Holy Spirit and speak in tongues. This was always the earth-shattering topic. What was the purpose then of being a Christian? There was no truth, no power, no extraordinary. The Bible to them was a compilation of great fables and metaphors. To me, it had become a life-giving river. It always baffled me that the same Christians had no problem believing in the supernatural powers of Satan and the demonic realm. They feared ever having anything to do with witches or Satanists. This made me crazy! How could they believe that the created was more powerful than the Creator?! Argument after argument, I felt like I was a defense attorney in federal court defending my client: the supernatural God of the Bible.

After these heated exchanges, I would get alone with God and tell Him I was sorry we had treated Him like that as a society, and that He deserved honor, reverence, and true worship from all of us. I asked Him why His supposed people all had begun to believe that He would no longer be like He was in the days of old. I could almost feel his desire to find someone that would rise up and be like the characters of the Bible, so that He again would be that God through them. I ran to the front of that spiritual line! As a result of these one on one conversations, I would repeatedly get on my knees and implore Him to use me to bring back His Kingdom and glorify his Name. I would end up prostrate on the floor in tears crying out for Him to please not pass me by! I told Him to do whatever he wanted to with my life, and that it was His now. I cried as I thought of not having the chance to live this great life along His side. There is nothing else I wanted more. These emotional exchanges would happen behind closed doors, with just me and Him. I wanted my life to impact His Kingdom. I wanted Him to look down from Heaven and smile at His new son, maybe even laugh over me with joy. I wanted Him to know that all the passion and dedication that I gave Satan when I was in his camp, were now completely at His disposal. I pleaded with Him to throw me in the front lines; I didn't care the cost. I wanted to raise the banner of His Name in the midst of His enemy's armies, because His enemies were now my enemies. Never had such zeal erupted from my heart. I had a worthy cause, and a worthy King. I knew God had heard my pleas and that in due time He would honor them. I had memorized the scripture verse about His eyes roaming to and fro over the earth to find someone to do His will. I felt like a stranded man on an island, building the monumental wood stack to light a fire to alert over passing planes of His presence, in an attempt to be rescued. I cried and yelled to make sure that those searching eyes of my God fixed on me during this quest to find willing sons for His cause. I was so excited to be His I wanted to scream in joy.

I wanted other Christians to wake up and smell the Kingdom. We were ambassadors of The King, not a king, The King! Eternity was ours as a gift from His merciful Throne. We had nothing to lose by taking this puff of smoke called the remainder of our lives and spilling it at His feet to do with as He pleased for His namesake. Did they really think they could find some more worthy cause to throw their life at? It drove me nutty seeing that Satanists were more dedicated to Satan than Christians were to God. Even worse, I saw the dedication all the other religions had from their patrons. We had the real God! The only one that saves! He actually loved us! I wanted to tear my hair out. I was going to be the voice of reason to speak loud in the midst of this insanity. I would awaken this sleeping crowd back to their God. This was my heart's desire. I set out on a quest to find others that wanted to share in my cause. I wanted to find fearless warriors, or at least those that were willing to be transformed into such by my God.

I will say, after nine plus years now of this wonderful new life, that one of the hardest things for me has been, and still is, interacting with lukewarm and uncommitted professed Christians. I have developed much more compassion for them now, as a result of God's grace, and discipline forming humility and love in me. But, my internal screams to ready ourselves for battle have not changed.

Chapter 22: My God Institutionalizes the Sane

Well, back to the story:

In the previous months I had been quite the busy little Kingdom bee. I had successfully been kicked out of a Baptist church, a small home church, and a larger church in a barn. This was not a result of me falling into debauchery or heresy. No, it was a result most of the time of my zealousness offending and making people uncomfortable. Sure I made mistakes, but who doesn't? My heart, though, was for Him and His people. I wanted to awaken them to the wonders of the Kingdom. Sometimes my tactics were quite aggressive, to say the least. What can I say? I was a zealot. How could I not be if I actually believed I was called by God for a purpose that carried eternal ramifications for all involved? It was here that my walk took its next step in the progression of me becoming the Godly man I am called to be.

A year before I was born again I had been unlucky enough as to become the target of an unscrupulous woman's scheme to frame me for sexual assault in an attempt to extort me financially. When I met God I was deeply involved in a lawsuit against a police department, a city, and multiple individuals that had slandered and destroyed my reputation. This suit initially had the potential of procuring millions of dollars to me for incurred damages. It wasn't days after I was born again that God told me to drop the whole thing. It was hard to do, but how could I say no after the mercy and grace that He had shown me? Later on, the people involved in a malicious attempt to retaliate because I was exposing their deviant plan recruited the help of someone they knew that worked at the attorney general's office. They set out on a campaign to again smear my name. This resulted in the licensing board issuing a hearing to hear the false accusations made against me. Long story short: the best they could come up with is that I had an extramarital sexual encounter years prior, that as a physician it was ethically wrong, and I needed to be sanctioned. Are you serious?! I was deeply entrenched in the "worldly" behavior of "physicians" back in the day. This crusade to attack me for something ridiculous that happened years prior was almost unbelievable.

Nonetheless, my attorney came up with an idea to offer a voluntary enrollment in a facility to assess my emotional and mental ability to operate ethically in society. This is the politically correct way to say I offered to put myself in a mental assessment facility and be scrutinized and prodded by a barrage of psychologists, psychiatrist, social workers, and counselors. Not to mention plenty of blood tests, urine screens and many other fun exploratory venues to establish that I was a functioning human. At first I was very reluctant to agree, but then I figured I really didn't care about all this anymore; after all, I was a fisherman now. I had wasted enough of my time fighting these ridiculous assaults against me. So, I said okay.

The paperwork was finalized, and now I had to find a location for this fun week to unfold. I prayed over and over about it, and felt like God told me to go to Kansas for it. Kansas?! I grew up in Italy. I barely knew where Kansas was. I made sure I had heard Him correctly, and once I was assured it was His will, I went and found a map of the US. Kansas was far! I had gone to chiropractic school in Chicago, and that was already pretty far from home, but Kansas was really far. I asked God if I could find a place in Chicago. I felt like a barterer in a flea market with God. His resolve was unyielding, for reasons I did not know, or understand, He wanted me in the far off land of Kansas. I eventually found a facility that qualified, made the appointment, and off Danielle and I went. It was around Christmas time.

As much as I hated having to be put through this emotionally and spiritually taxing process, I knew that there was some reason that the Lord had encouraged me to sign up for it. More importantly, I knew that it needed to take place in Kansas, no-where else. I was quite sure that it was not the geographical location of the facility, but the people there. It was during the next two to three days that I began to take a vested interest in the personal lives and personalities of the other guests there. I still was being subjected to all the segments of the plan myself, but I devoted a large amount of my thoughts and discernment to the state of the others. This process would eventually lead to a conflict with the group during one of our large group therapy sessions.

It was Thursday afternoon. Four grueling days of being prodded and poked had passed. The circular couch arrangement was full of semi-willing participants. An already abrasive conversation was well underway between all the other guests there. I, as always, was more intent on listening and processing with God than with the other people there. I felt a violent and angry stare begin to direct itself at me. One of the men there, a renowned medical professional, had locked eyes with me. I could see a severe level of agitation overtake him almost instantly. I was curious to know exactly what was going on inside his mind; a curiosity that was very short lived. In a verbal assault this man began to unleash accusation at me.

"So what, are too f###in' good to talk to us?"

He continued: "What, are you the only perfect f###in' one here?"

I was quite taken by surprise. I had only shared simple "good mornings" and "hellos" up to that point with him. I felt under siege. My reflexive response in the past would have directed me to attack in return, something I was really good at. But that day I was not the same man that had responded in that fashion countless times before. Something (or someone) was holding back the vengeful and insecure side of my emotions, allowing me to calmly address the heated questions posed to me. I went on to apologize for not participating more in the verbal exchanges in the room, and then I also told them why. I began to voice the fact that I did not agree with the therapeutic methods that they were trying to implement. I also explained to them that I did not feel there would be any success in producing the desired changes in their lives and their hearts by means of such pragmatic therapy. I had their undivided attention now!

There I was staring at a silent mob with apparent emotional and social deficiencies. The silent approach and aloof behavior I had hidden behind were instantly vanquished. They demanded me to offer more to validate my stance, I knew this for sure. How possibly do you tell a group of people you have just spent thirty hours with (in a very trying set of circumstances) that they are all demonized?! How do you try and explain to them the fact that they are under the curse of fallen creation and that they need to be born again?! I was quite used to being a public speaker, but this time it was just a tad different than any time before. It was in that moment that I voiced the question that has become a hallmark of my last nine and a half years:

"Do you really want to know why?"

I felt that question absolved me from some of the typical responses that would get thrown back at me. Usually severely discontent hearers of the words I would speak led to verbal and emotional lashings aimed at me. This time, I quickly received a general annoyed consensus from the small crowd and prepared to share. I began by telling them how messed up I was prior to the last two years. I also explained that I had tried any and all known socially approved therapeutic remedies for my thoughts, desires, and actions, but all to no avail. I went on to discredit common logic in the face of a greater way I had now encountered. They all seemed more attentive and less hateful as I went on. I began to tell them that I had finally found the answer, the only answer that could produce real change in a person's life, and that it was not perpetual therapy.

Craig Stasio

"Time's up for this session." Bellowed the director of this fun social excursion.

"Are you kidding me?!", I thought.

Was he really going to leave them hanging like that? The answer was yes, he was. I guess that left a curiosity that would help fill the couches at our next session later on that evening. I smiled at them and told them I would share the rest later. On to my next part of this all-consuming process.

I was escorted into a large personal office. I knew it was a personal office by the level of personalized décor and pictures within it. I knew that this was probably the "Head Man's" office.

"Well, here we go!" I thought.

The time of reckoning was here. I had long awaited response and opinion to the multiple questionnaires I had filled out on day one. All those questions about hearing voices in my head and about believing in angels and demons... I felt like this was going to be a one on one with the main person there, the one really in charge. This was confirmed when I was told to have a seat and wait for the head psychiatrist, the one who's name was at the top of all the business cards with numerous initials following. I braced myself for what I anticipated to be a confrontational exchange where my very faith and beliefs were about to be challenged. I knew that this conversation would be the most pivotal one. The results of this coming conversation would deeply affect the staff's decision on what to write in the report to follow my stay at their facility. This fact (or fact bereft) compilation of conjecture and subjective opinions would deeply affect my life in the natural upon my return home to Michigan. I felt almost at the mercy of their dictates. A touch of fear and worry seemed to be sprinkled on me from a deviant overhead shaker. I felt the suffocating spiritual vice began to constrict my heart and my faith. Voices in my head began an all-out assault on me with emotion bullets. The goal was to push me to yield to unbelief in an attempt at self-preservation. I could feel myself wanting to shrink back from the new beliefs and faith I had acquired in the past year. I knew that if I just submitted to whatever was put before me that it would be a far less bumpy road for me.

It was in that moment that a fiery zeal arose within me. I was not going to throw away my faith to achieve some level of social comfort or aristocratic acceptance. What I had found in Jesus was priceless; I was not willing to have it bartered over like an exotic scarf at a flea market. My choice was final, I would stand my spiritual ground at any cost.

"Hello Mr. Stasio" erupted from the otherwise silent hallway leading into the office. The last name basis greeting: one of the things that I always hated to either give or receive. It was society's attempt to put up dividing social and emotional walls. But what I really hated about it was that it always demanded an impersonal response in return. Usually this kind of greeting would be followed by an introduction as doctor so and so, or councilman so and so, all which were nothing more than attempts at handing me a verbal hand fan to fuel the flame of their pride. I responded with a simple greeting, "good afternoon".

I could see the somewhat puzzled look on his face as he sat down behind the large oak desk and began to open the folder in front of him. I am sure that inside that folded manila colored paper were all the results of my tests and private sessions. While he appeared in the natural to be going over them before opening a dialogue with me, I could tell that his mind was focused on something else. He quickly closed the file and looked at me quite attentively. I could tell that most people to him where simply a means to an end. This clinic was known for its discretion, which attracted people of high society, or ample financial means, to enroll for therapy. I could tell, though, that for many it was more of a glorified timeout session resulting from some sort of misbehavior in the sight of the populous. This facility served as a way for them to be allowed re-acclimation among the people they had wronged. The staff's approval after a prolonged stay would usually allow for a level of mercy to be extended towards the accused upon their return home.

There I was, the next person for him to put a stamp of approval or denial upon. His eyes locked on mine for a brief moment of silence as he prepared to speak. Usually the people brought before him would hang on every word he spoke. They would appear to be frazzled and intimidated by the power he held in his hand and his pen in regards to the future of their lives. He was used to this very predictable response from all those unlucky enough to be scrutinized by society to the point of ending up there. The silence seemed quite uncomfortable but it gave me a chance to listen clearly to God speak to me as how to proceed. I could discern a great level of interest stirring inside the man. As had happened so many times before, I could feel the stirring in the spiritual atmosphere around us. God was doing something; His hands were absolutely involved with whatever was about to take place. I became quite excited and at the same time a level of nervousness seemed to have joined my other emotions. I am sure the environment and the impending circumstances were the cause for this.

"Mr. Stasio, I have been watching you now for close to a week. I have never seen a person here act like you have."

What an opening to our conversation. This dialogue could now be headed in any direction. The fact that I could feel the presence of God there was the only thing that gave me assurance it was not headed down a nasty path. The inflections of his voice told me that when he said that he had been watching me, that he was relaying that an extraordinary level of attentiveness had been allocated to me. However it had happened, I had gained this man's interest, and now I would probably find out why God had set up all the circumstances for this to occur.

"I have watched you interacting with all the people in the group therapy sessions, and I have never seen someone be so peaceful through the process. It almost seemed as if you were wrapped in absolute peace, even when the others verbally assaulted you without cause."

Although this most recent phrase came out of his mouth as a statement it really was being offered as an inferred question. What he really was saying was that he wanted me to tell him how it was that I could maintain a position of emotional serenity in that most unsettling scene. Truth be told, I think that he wanted desperately to know the answer to that so that he could apply it to his own life. I could see a level of brokenness in his eyes. Life seemed to have not yielded the answers to him he had so desperately sought out and felt like he deserved. I am sure a man like him that spends day after day immersed in emotional typhoons is overtaken by a level of hopelessness for the human race. The missing link to the puzzle that his mind had been trying to solve for so long is understood that the root of all he observes is spiritual. All the natural manifestations and emotional outbursts are nothing more than people responding to spiritual realities happening around and within them.

I could tell that there was a pause offered after this most recent statement. He was allowing, and wanting me to offer, answers to questions he was not supposed to ask in this setting. After all, he was the head clinician there. He was supposed to be the one with all the answers. Showing any sign of weakness or pure curiosity would have been damaging to his self-created image. I knew that he could tell that I had the real answer to all the problems ravaging the hearts and minds of his patients. He had finally found the vaccine to all the diseases plaguing his life and all the other lives entrusted into his clinical hands. The answers he had sought out for so long were right there in front of him. Finally he could not hold back the question any longer:

"I have never seen someone so peaceful here. How is it that you are able to stay in such a state of peace to where nothing happening around you seems to rattle you?"

There it was, the question I knew was eating at him. I felt like a switch had happened as if we had suddenly swapped positions at the desk. I was quite sure this man was not used to humbling himself to a state of allowing others to speak into his life, so I knew this was a very special moment for him. I quickly tried to hear how God wanted to use this open door to minister to this precious man. My response to him was simple: "Do you really want to know how I am able to stay so peaceful?"

Truth be told, I was concerned about what a full disclosure answer would result in for me. After all, he was about to make an imposing decision on the status of my mental and social capacities to the authoritative figures in my life, or should I say, my past life. But as it was now in my newfound life and reality, I really did not care so much about potential ramifications for my words or actions prompted by God and my new Christian life and faith. I swiftly began to tell the attentive man before me that I had found God. He did not offer the response you would usually expect from a man in his position. He did not seem startled or appalled by my answer; it was almost as if he expected exactly that. I went on to tell him of my experience in the basement and of all that had happened to me up to my arrival in Kansas.

I shared with him that in one of my sessions at his facility, while they were trying to convince me to yield to a higher authority as part of a twelve step process, I told the psychologist that I already had. I also told him that the only one that they should yield to was Jesus. I told him that creating other Gods to yield to as part of a recovery process would only lead to them becoming more demonized and distraught. I could see such a level of suppressed excitement swirling inside that man's soul as I continued to disclose my Christian experiences. He really was interested in what I had to say, but I was really not sure as to why just yet, except that I knew that God had arranged this very discussion. At the conclusion of my story I paused to allow the man a chance to respond or to do whatever the temporary silence prompted him to do. After a short period of internal reflection he spoke:

"I used to believe in God. I even became a Catholic priest for years. But I never found God there. Eventually this led me to lose my faith and I turned to science instead, and became a psychiatrist."

I could feel pain and shame begin to rise up within him as he spoke. Humility began to manifest within this broken man as I watched the reality of my words and my God offer a renewed hope for him. I offered him grace and mercy along with encouragement. I told him that the real God was always there for him, but that he was not found within the doctrine of Catholicism, for most of their creeds were nothing but empty religion. The living God was still completely available for him and wanted him back. I began to prophesy to him words that shook him to his core. I could see and feel the impact this conversation had on this man. As our conversation ended he offered me a thankful handshake, but it was more than apparent that what he wanted to offer was a gratitude bearing hug.

The meeting would eventually end and it was time again for lunch. This day though, I knew that God wanted me to spend lunch with the other people there and not to leave the facility, so I did. Go figure: who I would be seated next to at lunch? Yep, the man accusing me in the previous session. Well, there I was again in another situation to show the love of God to a broken down person in desperate need of Him. I was so grateful to have real hope in me while being surrounded by so much hopelessness. I really wanted to offer others the wonder of salvation that I had been granted. I could tell that he anxiously waited to see my response to him sitting next to me. I could tell that he, too, knew that I was different from the others there. He wanted the peace I had but did not know how to ask for help, so instead he lashed out emotionally in his pain. I quickly began a simple dialogue that led to a more profound exchange between us. As the stream of our conversation merged to the topic of God the others at the table seemed to be caught in the net of intrigue. Many surrounding ears listened as this fisher of men began to share the oracles of God. The physical food of lunch began to lose its appeal to all the people there as the treasures of God's Kingdom were laid out on the spiritual table before them.

I befriended the man that sat next to me and at the end of the day was privileged enough to pray for him. I had found out that this poor man had been coming there for years trying to rid himself of a passionate anger that had consumed his life and his medical practice. Finally, he had tasted real peace. A victim of severe repeated abuse was also overcome by the grace of God and received a level of freedom from her emotional woundedness. I was so happy to be a messenger of God's grace to the broken people there. All of a sudden the long drive and large bill did not seem that important any more. Unlike natural fishing, any day you return with a net of even one you had an incredibly good day! God had used me in this dark and hopeless place to lead some to real peace only found in Him. That night my wife and I went into town and scavenged around until we found a bookstore that sold Christian books. We purchased whatever books we felt the Lord led us to for the people there. We were so excited to be part of the grand Kingdom mission from God. Our lives were His to use as He saw fit to, even if it was to minister in a mental assessment and treatment center in Kansas. What a life!

Dark circumstances could always be turned into victorious events of celebration once the Kingdom and the King made their presence known.

The entire process would end that Friday with the staff wanting to meet my wife. She came in and shared her powerful testimony, and collaborated the stories about mine. They were all quite intrigued by the awesome stories of our salvation. Eventually handshakes and goodbyes would release us back into the world again. The whole process had been a tremendous victory for the Kingdom. I was very happy at how it all turned out. These were the awesome events that took place during the mornings and afternoon hours that unforgettable week in Kansas. But now let me share with you the even crazier events that took place in the evenings and very early morning hours.

Chapter 23: Those Crazy Kansas Nights

After a long fourteen-hour car ride we had arrived in the state of Kansas at approximately 3 am on Sunday morning. We checked in to a hotel and slept until noon. Once awake we sought food, but more importantly, I sought answers from God as to why I was in Kansas. We ended up eating at a local well-known chain restaurant next to the hotel. I prayed in tongues and English under my breath at the table trying to get God to disclose some breadcrumbs of understanding as to why He so adamantly wanted me in Kansas. As we were awaiting the food we ordered my wife had brought a magazine from the hotel and began to scour through it to find local church services and found a listing on the back page. One of them had a 5 pm service; we had missed all others. We were sure this was not a coincidence. I asked for the bill and told my wife that we were about to go on another God excursion. We exited the restaurant and made our way to the car in anticipation of whatever God had in plan for us, absolutely convinced that He was involved. We drove off to the church based on directions from the waitress. We quickly arrived at the intersection where we were told the church was located, but there was nothing around but fast food chain restaurants. I was confused. I felt for sure that God wanted me to visit the local Presbyterian church found in that magazine. But here I was with no church in view. I looked around attentively to see if maybe it was located off in the backdrop of any of the viewable buildings, but still nothing.

I then noticed a man standing there alone on the street, and I decided to ask him if he could help us find this church. I rolled down my window to ask the simple question. As he turned in my direction to respond I could tell that there was something incredibly wrong with him. I was not sure about what was happening, but I knew before he even spoke that this man was absolutely demon possessed. The man bellowed out a deep toned response to my question laced with profanity and annoyance. He stated that there was no such church anywhere around that location. I quickly rolled up my window, looked at my wife, and began to pray. Sometimes still to this very day when I find myself in need of answers I forget the all-important fact: I know God! I rapidly turn from questioning people to praying to Him. I asked the Lord to show me where this church was. After all, He was really the one directing me to go there. The answer came to me immediately. How foolish I felt in that moment, knowing that all I had to do is ask Him and then listen for the answer. What a simple concept so many of us Christians always seem to lose from our memories.

"Honey, the church is down that little road off to the left." I shared with my wife.

She, in turn, asked how I knew that. My look back at her was all the answer she would ever need. She was quite accustomed to my communicating practices with God by now. Her silent look back at me was as to say: "Here we go again", as a subtle smile overtook her face. It was not more than a quarter mile down the road where we came to find the very church we had felt like we were supposed to visit. To my surprise the parking lot was empty, that is, except for one small car parked next to the front door. This was not the main service, but an evening Bible study, but surely more people would be coming than just us? I parked my car next to the only other one there and me and my wife opened the front door. As we entered the very silent building we started to make our presence known by shouting a pleasant "hello". It did not take long for us to receive a response. Out of a back small room a 50 year old man came forth to greet us. For the sake of this book we will call him Al. As he approached us I spoke before any questions or statements could be offered:

"Hi, God sent us here!"

What an icebreaker. At least I was in a church, not the soon to come mental assessment center. For sure I thought that a statement like that would not only be received in this place, but validated. Neither of these would be the case. The man introduced himself as the pastor, and appeared to have a severe level of agitation to my statement. I quickly offered up that I was a minister of the gospel, a fisher of men, as I thought he was. And that God had sent me there by the leading of the Holy Spirit. His responses were saturated in unbelief. Not only an unbelief that questioned my statements, but also the very ability for God to do something like send somebody across the U.S. to a seemingly random church. He then went on to share with me that he did not believe in such things as the baptism of the Holy Spirit, or speaking in tongues. I was taken aback and disappointed, but more than that I was frustrated and angry at his response. I was still suffering emotionally from the wounds inflicted on me from the Baptist church and the other Christians back home that constantly persecuted me for my faith. Surely God did not need to send me to Kansas to find another minister that lacked almost any faith in the reality of my God and the supernatural capabilities of His Kingdom to manifest in present day America. Somehow the church must have thought that the constitution wrote off God's ability to still be God! After this opening discourse, in a moment of emotional turmoil I excused myself from him and exited the building. I stood outside the door and began to pray.

"Lord, I don't want to do this again. He doesn't even believe in the real You. But I know You sent me here, so if You really still want me to talk to him, I will. Please give me a sign to encourage me to go back in there and to battle the unbelief inside him."

The sign I specifically asked for was for a bird to appear next to me. As I finished the brief prayer I looked up to the sky as if to petition Heaven to please answer me as soon as possible. In less than five seconds, while my gaze was still directed in the direction of His Throne in the heavens, my answer came. Right above me a small bird appeared from the roof of the building and as it approached even to the edge of the overhanging gutter it leaned towards me with an intense stare. As if that was not enough it began to wildly chirp like I had never seen such a creature do. What could I do now?! I knew I was supposed to go in and continue what God had ultimately started in there.

After all, I felt like I had just been both encouraged and rebuked by the Lord through the beak of a small bird. My resolve now was absolute. No matter what he said or how religious he was about to be I would make my case to him about the reality of my God, and my Christian walk.

The conversation became quite uncomfortable as the exchanges of polar opposite views went on. My wife sat back and watched silently, but quite attentively. Finally, there appeared to be somewhat of a spiritual breakthrough. He acknowledged to me that he would not change his stance on his unbelief, but that if I wanted I could go and talk to his wife at his house. He stated that she had also had many of these conversations with him about the spirit realm, and speaking in tongues as well. He told me that maybe I would find it more enjoyable to share my stories with her, but that he was busy preparing for his teaching. Go figure, God sends you a messenger and you ignore him to prepare another religious study.

My frustration at that time with most other Christians was monumental. (Little did I know at that time about all my flaws and shortcomings in the things of God.) Nevertheless, my state of frustration with the minister was apparent. Back in my car I went. My car pulled out of the parking lot and my frustration spilled out to my wife. She encouraged me as she usually did. What a gift that woman has been to my life, my walk, and my children. We decided to let go of my frustration and to instead focus on the next task at hand, talking to his wife. I had no idea as what to expect from my next God encounter, except that it would probably go over a little better than the last one. I arrived ten minutes later to a medium sized residence in the middle of a quaint, middle class community. I knocked on the colorful, decorative front door awaiting this next step of my walk to begin. A woman answered the door with a large and genuine smile. I introduced myself in the same way I did with her husband:

"Hi, God sent us here."

The perfect icebreaker. The ultimate climate shifter and spiritual statement to cut through all the typical religious pleasantries. Her response was not the one I expected:

"Great! Come on in! We are about to worship, join in with us."

"Awesome!" I thought.

Finally some non-resistance to my God overtures. My wife began to take off her jacket and offered it to the woman of the house so she could hang it up. As I began to enter the living room a man appeared from down the hallway and greeted me with a very unusual statement.

"This is a divine appointment of the Lord. And He said to give these to you."

In his hands was a twelve CD compilation of teachings from the International House of Prayer (also known as IHOP, and which we had never heard of before) on encountering Jesus. With a silent smile I accepted this great gift. I was now at ease. I was surrounded by other crazy Christians like us. Within minutes we were seated in the large living room and introduced to her two teenage daughters as they began to take their place at a piano and behind a large exotic drum set. Their mother grabbed a guitar and the man a tambourine of sorts. A large box of other instruments were placed at our feet and Danielle and I were told to help ourselves to any of them if we wanted to. A spontaneous worship session began with power. We felt an immediate presence of the Lord overtake that room as me and my wife kneeled and began weeping as we felt the love of God overtake us. We then gratefully began to join in the worship as we sang along with our newfound brethren. What a great day.

After about an hour and a half of some of the most beautiful worship we had ever been a part of we sat together and shared our testimonies with each other. We were seated with like Christians: radically converted, previously heathen, set free by the power of the Cross. We talked for hours. Eventually they needed to leave for a youth meeting they had previously scheduled, so we decided to go back to our hotel room. The man there (who we will call Bo) invited me to spend time with him the next evening, if I was free. I shared with them that I was stuck in the counseling sessions until 6 pm that Monday through Friday, but that I would love to meet up after that. He agreed.

Off we went back to the hotel, me and my precious wife, both so happy we had decided to come to Kansas at the leading of the Lord without having really known any reason why beforehand. We replayed the day's events and were so excited to have found other Christians like us that we could talk plainly to without having to gage what level of our real lives they could relate to. What a peaceful night's sleep we expected now that we had received such a refreshing touch from God.

The next night after the sessions at the counseling center I met up with Bo. We talked until about midnight. At the end of the night he invited me to come and meet his friend, who was a prophet, the next morning. I told him that I would love to, but that I had to go into the facility at 9 am. He said that would not be a problem, because his friend had to leave for work by 6:30 am, so we would plan to meet him at about 5 am.

"Absolutely!" belted out of my mouth.

Craig Stasio

I was so excited to be part of any God venture that sleep held a very small level of importance in my life (and still does). I went back to the hotel and told my wife that I was getting back up at 4:30 am to meet Bo again to go see his prophet friend. She smiled at me, voicing her subtle concerns for my lack of sleep, especially in lieu of the taxing week ahead of me. We embraced and went to bed. I was so excited about the potential meeting with a prophet that I did know if I could even go to sleep.

The early morning alarm bellowed in the dark silence of the room. It seemed as though I had just shut my eyes mere minutes ago. The excitement of the impending encounter outweighed the physical deprivation. I was up and dressed in minutes. A soft and sincere kiss was offered my still sleeping wife, and off to meet Bo I went. As a simple gesture of friendship Bo brought me a much-appreciated cup of early morning coffee. I got into his car and off to meet his friend we went. I really had no idea what to expect from a meeting with a real prophet. Truth be told I didn't care, I just wanted to know anyone that knew my God. I knew that they were the only ones I could really relate to at that point of my life. Also, I wanted to learn as much about my God as I could so I wanted to probe the minds and hearts of all those that knew Him.

We arrived at the prophet's house at about 5 am and he and his wife were at the kitchen table having a cup of coffee of their own. We were introduced, and testimonies were exchanged.

After about 30 minutes Bo's friend asked if we could all stand together and pray. Sounded good to me. So we all arose from the table and joined hands in the kitchen area. I was about to pray with a prophet! How exciting is that?! Again not knowing what to expect I filled with nervous anticipation. The three of us began to pray first, allowing for the prophet to go last. As it got to be his turn I could feel a deep intensifying presence of God fill that small home. The man began to pray in a powerful way, one I was not accustomed to seeing others do. As he prayed I could feel the Holy Spirit stirring in our midst. I could also tell that the level of anointing on that man and the conviction of his words was escalating rapidly. He began to shake violently and weep. I was overcome by the moment as I froze in anticipation.

I humbled myself before God and his servant the prophet. The word to come out of him I will never forget:

"Lord! It is so much, will he be able to stand?!"

And "Lord, give him grace so he does not fall!"

Pleadingly he continued, "Lord give him grace!"

You can only imagine what went on inside me. Fear, joy, excitement, just to name a few emotions. Although I was overcome on the inside I did not dare interrupt this most holy moment. No, I stood silently and waited for an acceptable time to voice my questions. Eventually the prophet stopped shaking and crying and released my hand as he looked at me with a great big smile. He shared what he had seen while he was praying for me. He stated that the Lord had given him a vision of me on a beach. All of a sudden the ocean began to stir. Waves started to come in towards the shore washing up to my feet. Then all of a sudden the waves got bigger and more powerful hitting against me as I stood firm and unmoved on that shore. He then looked off in the distance and saw incredibly large tidal waves headed in my direction. It was during that part of the vision that he cried out: "Lord! It is so much will he be able to stand?" He then came out of the vision shaking and weeping under the anointing of the Holy Spirit. At first I was so speechless I did not know what to ask. My biggest question was: what did the waves represent? And what exactly did it mean for me not to fall? More importantly, I was trembling with fear of the Lord as to what potential "falling" would mean.

Before I could seek verbal counsel from the prophet he began to answer my unspoken questions and concerns. He went on to tell me that the Lord was showing him that I was called as a minister and that the waves represented people that the Lord was going to send into my life and into the ministry he entrusted me with in future years. A quick sigh of internal relief swept peacefully over my heart and soul. Fear turned immediately to hope and excitement! I left that morning super encouraged and returned to my hotel room to shower and prepare for my counseling extravaganza.

Night after night we met up with Bo and the pastor's wife and daughters to have incredible Godly fellowship. The wife (who we will call Tina) had shared with me and my wife that the Lord had called her to be a missionary minister to third world countries. She also shared that her husband was absolutely against it. She shared her internal struggles with the fact that he was so full of unbelief in regards to the supernatural things of the Kingdom and the Holy Spirit. We did what we could to offer her comfort and encouragement. We could tell this enigma was ripping her apart at the seams and putting a tremendous strain on their marriage and their family. She invited us to stay for dinner one night with her and her husband. All of the other evenings we were there her husband would come home and cordially slip into the basement or his room to try and avoid us at any cost. After all, we were more of the crazy Christians like his wife. Tina thought that God wanted us to have a dinner alone with her and her husband and we agreed.

That evening we arrived with a bottle of wine, not knowing exactly how to present ourselves for a dinner such as this. There he was, seated on the couch. I could discern he was there more as a favor to his wife than because he really wanted to fellowship with us. At first that made me a little uncomfortable, but as I began to talk about my Creator and Savior I got over it. We tried to share testimonies with her husband but it did not go over very smooth. Tina gave a call to fill the table as dinner was ready, relieving us all from the uncomfortable tension of the previous conversation. The actual dinner was quite uneventful, after which we re-gathered on the couches to again converse. It was then that the Lord decided to have me pierce the religious bubble around that man. I looked right at him and said: "The Lord has told me, to tell you, he wants you to speak in tongues." His response was that of a severely agitated man:

"Now you have upset me. When you say things like 'the Lord has talked to you' it upsets me. Because the Lord does not talk to people, you cannot hear Him like that."

You would think that this would shut me down, or at least cause me to pause and shrink back from any such future statements but that is not what happened. I had heard his response, but the unction of the Holy Spirit inside me was far greater than any external resistance. I continued: "The Lord also says that he is going to baptize you in the Holy Spirit."

The man became infuriated! It was so crazy to see a pastor (or should I say Presbyterian minister) respond to my words like that. Then he shut down emotionally, saying something that has stuck with me for years: "Can't we share the things we commonly agree upon and not the thing we disagree about?"

While I was sure it was the Lord leading me to confront the religious moat surrounding that man's castle, those words pierced me. The conversation was tapered down by him, and eventually he nicely asked me and my wife to leave in so many words. I left somewhat sad from that encounter. Deep down though, I knew the Lord was trying to reach that man and bring him into the deep things of the gospel and the Kingdom. We returned to our hotel, and days later, back to Michigan and all the spiritual things awaiting our return.

Chapter 24: My Path Confirmed; Stepping Out of the Boat

Upon returning to our normal life back home (if normal could really even apply any more) we were encouraged and ready to continue our faith walk. I really wanted to share with our Christian friends all the experiences we had in Kansas. Sad to say, they were not in the least bit interested in what we received out in Kansas. As a matter of fact, they seemed quite annoyed with us. They seemed jealous for some reason that I did not understand at the time. I still tried to convey to them my zealous beliefs in the Kingdom, and in living a Kingdom life here and now. I could see them so caught up in their temporal lives that it made me crazy. Didn't they know we were sons and daughters of God?! We had a real purpose now, much higher than anything else we could ever do in this life before we knew God. We had the Holy Spirit inside us! We could impact people's lives for eternity: yes, eternity! My zealous overtures meant to encourage and empower were usually met with varying levels of resistance. I wanted so badly for the people around me to abandon themselves to the reality of Jesus and His Kingdom. But the acts and functions of everyday life seemed to claim far more of their attention. By this point they had stopped inviting me to their group functions and when I confronted them about it they said that all I did was talk about God and that I needed to give it a break. What?! Are you serious?! Unfortunately, this was the case. I was distraught. These were the people that were supposed to teach me and help raise me up in the things of God. What was I supposed to do? I was so confused and scared on how to proceed.

So I got on my knees and cried out to my Father for help. I was so torn inside. I felt with every ounce of me that Jesus had saved me and commissioned me as a minister of the gospel, the real gospel. One full of power and love, one that saved, one that restored, and one that was as radical as the God it came from. Yet, here I was surrounded by so many that did not share these views. It had gotten to the point that I was attacked by the leaders in our fellowship for praying for people to get born again, which was happening on a daily basis at the office and anywhere else the Lord would allow me to. This was met with utter resistance from others in the group. I was even told that I was ruining other people's faith and relationship with God by praying for them to receive the Holy Spirit baptism too early. Are you kidding me?! I was left speechless. I could not even begin to understand such a statement. When I asked for clarification I was reminded that I had financial debt in my name, and that my attention needed to be directed toward that instead; also, that as long as I had debt it was irresponsible for me to focus on ministry. What was I supposed to do? I had in excess of 1.5 million dollars of outstanding debt from previous businesses going bad and gambling related debts along with a destructive lifestyle prior to meeting God. I was invested heavily in trying to become a business mogul and author right before I was born again, all of which I walked away from once I met God. It was impossible in the natural for me to pay such enormous debts. They even went to the extent of telling me I was in rebellion for praying for people to get Spirit filled in lieu of my financial state.

I locked myself away and fell to my knees before my God. I prayed for clarity and some sort of supernatural confirmation to what I felt God was leading me to do with my life. I cried frustrated tears before my Father. All I wanted to do was please Him. I wasn't interested in the public's opinion of me, just His. After many prayers and tears my resolve was renewed to tear down the kingdom of darkness and proclaim the Kingdom of my Lord Jesus the Christ.

I confronted the accusatory voices rising up all around me. I asked them how was it that if I was in rebellion, that the people I prayed for to get born again and Spirit filled were getting exactly that, born again and Holy Spirit filled. I declared that I had no authority in and of myself to do things in the Kingdom. I also told them if I was not in God's will then why was His Spirit constantly testifying of my behalf by manifesting His power through me? This was all met with even more resistance that was now becoming resentment. I was at the end of myself. I decided to keep walking in the faith I had and to keep following the leading of the Holy Spirit regardless of all the accusing and condemning voices rising up and shouting around me.

It was another Sunday morning in my new Christian life when the Lord decided to give me the awesome word of encouragement and confirmation I had pleaded to Him for. A worldwide known evangelist and teacher named John Bevere was coming to one of the churches in our area that day to speak. He is one of the main ministers that the people in my group at that time catered their teachings around, somewhat of a baseline for many of their doctrines and beliefs. I knew this was a big day for them to come and see him preach live, and careful preparations had been made to attend. My wife and I really wanted to see him, too. We had recently met a new sister in the Lord and felt like God wanted us to take her with us to that service. I arrived fifteen minutes or so early. As I entered the large church I could see our home fellowship, seated to the right hand side about fifteen rows back. My first inclination was to go sit next to them with my new sister even while fully expecting them to attack and criticize anything I said or did. As I began to prepare myself emotionally for such an event the Holy Spirit inside me began to whisper for me to go to the front row.

"What?!"

Certainly, the front row was reserved for all the ministers and important people at that very large church. I looked and saw the ropes sectioning off those seats as reserved. As if the rope was not enough, the taped signs with the large print word (RESERVED) washed away any doubt to the intentions of the people placing the ropes. Just as doubt to what I had heard began to creep in, the voice spoke again:

"Sit in the front row."

Now I was sure it was God. I had no idea how it was going to happen, I just knew it was. I had clearly heard a specific directive from my Father. I grabbed my wife's hand and gestured for her and the other woman to follow me. I made a beeline to the front row in full assurance of faith that God wanted me there for some reason. As I arrived I could see people all around preparing for the speaking of this mighty man of God. As I looked around again, there they were: three seats with no reserved marker on them. I knew those seats were for us with everything in me. I directed us to them and we graciously and meekly sat down. I looked over at the other people from our group and could see the distain in their eyes at me having the gall to sit in the front row. Even so, I knew God wanted me exactly there for a reason I did not know…at least not yet. The people from the church hierarchy and all the other ministers and their families took their places around the three of us.

We were immersed in questioning stares as to how we got those seats, but no one dared voice the question. A deep breath or two later we were settled and prepared for the service. I prepared to see why the Lord had me sit in the front row. I knew this day would bring clarity one way or the other to my walk: either through validation and encouragement, or through rebuke. Either way, I wanted closure and peace within myself that I was doing the Lord's will.

Craig Stasio

At 11 am began a beautiful worship set. I felt so humble there in the presence of my God. I still did not know why I was sitting in that front row but I was just happy to be His. I worshipped Him with my heart and soul. Sometimes, I felt so alone as I walked with other Christians; but that all was washed away when I entered His presence. He loved me, He really loved me. I was accepted and welcome in his Kingdom no matter what others thought of me. Outside of my wife and my children, unconditional love and acceptance was as rare as lightening hitting the same spot twice, even among fellow Christians.

The songs would end and there was a short pause leading up to the announcer welcoming John Bevere to the stage. He had been seated somewhat near to us with his family during the worship. I remembered looking at him and so desperately wanting God to use me like he used him for His Kingdom. To the natural eye he seemed like just another man, but in the spirit this was a giant raised by God to deliver the masses from deception and spiritual death. I watched him approach the pulpit in jeans, a simple sports jacket and tennis shoes. What a refreshing sight for me; so many times I watched men and women of God put more devotion into their apparel than into their message. This man made it all seem so simple. His demeanor was humble, yet he was utterly confident in his position in the Kingdom. With eager ears I waited to hear the message. And with a hurting heart I prayed for comfort.

The message offered that morning was from one of John's most recent books at that time, Living for Eternity. I had watched some of the teachings on that book as part of our Wednesday Bible study fellowship. The message outlined the reality of how small our time on this earth was compared to the eternal consequence our decisions and lives will bring about at the judgement seat of Jesus. It was a call to arms for the body of Christ to rise up to the challenge and sell out for the heavenly cause of proclaiming the coming of the Kingdom and our King! He emphasized the great choice we could make to live our lives completely for God, without fear or concern for self, assuring all the people there and the ones that would later see the television recording of this event, that it would be more than worth it. It was in that very moment that I felt a tremendous presence of the Holy Spirit come over me. I looked to my wife to see if she could discern the powerful and immediate shift in the spirit, I could tell that she absolutely could. I was not sure at all what this meant, but adrenaline started to release into my blood. I knew something really big was about to take place. I looked over to John Bevere who at that moment was walking away to my right about 30 or 40 seats away from me, his eyes looking in the other direction. My heart began to race even more as a spiritual door seemed to open around me. In that very instant John stopped speaking and stood still. I knew that whatever was occurring with me had now somehow captivated him as well. I really was not sure how many other people there were even aware of this event - I was too freaked out to care.

I saw John look up almost as if he were receiving a message from God right from Heaven above. I was terrified at the possibility of God taking that moment to publically rebuke me in front of the thousands there. I pondered that possibility and chose to resign myself to it; after all, I really wanted to please my God more than anything else. If a rebuke was needed to get me back on the right path I would try and embrace it as best I could without emotionally falling apart. I braced myself for the unknown to come as in a very rhythmic motion John Bevere turned around on his heels and still in complete silence looked directly at me. The level of emotions rose to all-time high inside of me. I could tell that God had communicated something to him, and now I knew that it was definitely something having to do with me. As if staring at me was not enough, John began to walk in my direction. You really have no idea what those seconds that felt like hours were like for me. There would be no avoiding what was about to happen. I had wanted truth and confirmation from God as to whether I was in His will or not. And now here he was sending John Bevere with the answer, and in front of a colossal crowd nonetheless. Not to mention, the whole thing was being recorded for television.

John approached my seat and finally stopped right in front of me. I was surprised that I did not pass out from the anxiety of the moment. The thing that kept me functional is that I knew without any doubt that this was God. No matter what happened next I knew that it would be for my good, and that it was something sent from my Father who deeply loved me. John stared right into my eyes and asked me what my name was.

"Craig."

That was all I could muster up to say at that moment. I was utterly star struck that God was doing this for me. John's eyes pierced mine even deeper than before as he asked me a simple question, at least that is what I thought when I first heard it:

"Do you know how awesome this is all going to be?"

My response was quick and given from a sincere heart:

"Yes, John, I do!"

To my dismay he looked at me and smiled and then looked up towards Heaven again and this time he spoke to our common Father:

"Lord, he doesn't understand!"

He then again turned his stare to me and again asked me:

"Craig, do you understand how awesome this is all going to be?"

Surely my first answer was not the right one, otherwise the question would not be asked again. I again answered as honestly as I knew how:

"John, I thought that I did."

John smiled even brighter than before and again raised his eyes to speak to the Lord right in front of me:

"Lord, he still doesn't understand!"

He then turned for the third time to ask me yet again:

"Craig, do you understand how awesome this is all going to be?!"

Now the Peter experience was complete with the third asking of the same question to which, like Peter, I knew I really did not have the complete answer.

"John, I guess I don't..."

What a humbling moment. But what an awesome moment as well. John got closer to me and placed his hands on my shoulders, looked right into my eyes, and spoke again:

"Mark my words Craig: me and you are going to be standing together in Heaven one day laughing about this very moment!"

I was undone. This mighty man of God had told me that one day I was going to end up in Heaven. The rest of the sentence was great but that part alone pierced my heart and brought me to tears. Another encouraging token from my faithful Father for his hurting son. That simple sentence meant so much to me. It blessed me in ways my emotions and words could never describe to you. I was still God's! I was still in His will! The message at that service was the very thing I had been trying to convey to all the people around me, seemingly to no avail. But now, there I was, not alone with that message. There was another man of God sent to confirm the message given to me from the Lord. And John Bevere nonetheless!

I then realized that all the people there that were part of my group of Christians had seen the events unfold. I thought for sure that this would lessen the attacks and persecution against me and my message of living recklessly for God. (This was all nice thinking on my part: the exact opposite occurred. I was resented even more after John talked to me by the leading of the Holy Spirit. I just could not believe this was happening to me.) The service would eventually come to an end and as I exited the building God put the cherry on the spiritual sundae He had just given me. An elderly stranger came up to me and put his hand on my shoulder:

"You are the one John talked to, right?"

Although the gentleman appeared to be offering a question I already knew that he knew the answer.

"Yes, that was me."

I responded with a simple genuine smile as I again relived the acceptance in God that beautiful moment had provided for me.

"You do what he said!"

As he smiled as brightly as any 70 year old man ever had and walked away from me full of joy. I pondered what exactly that meant. Then it occurred to me the message was to live an abandoned life on earth serving God and His Kingdom. The very message I was screaming to anyone who would listen.

The following week a large corporate gathering was held at what you would call our home church's headquarters, which happened to be in a large barn operating as a flea market. I remember the meeting culminating with a speaker passing around the microphone to anyone that had something to say. I felt compelled to speak as I grabbed the mic. I told the crowd that we now in this realm all look to the apostles and all the saints that have gone before us in awe, wishing so much that we could be with them now. But then I told them those very saints in Heaven wish they could have one more chance to come back and be given another chance to live this natural human life with all they know now having seen their Creator face to face. They wish they could come back and live a more dedicated and radical life for God, or should I say, with God. I went on to tell them that we still had the chance to do the very thing those saints wish they could. We were still here on earth. Surrounded by a fallen creation, yet so full of resurrection life inside us. We were ambassadors to the greatest Kingdom there would ever be. Announcing the coming of a glorious eternal King. Sure, I have heard of the reward the saints get at the bema seat of Jesus, where all our works are tested by the refiner's fire. Sure, I have read that all the works that make it through this testing because they were done for His glory will result in an eternal reward for us in Heaven. But, that was not the motivating factor in my zealous speech to help empower my brothers to live this radical Christianity. Truth is, Jesus saved me from impending eternal death and suffering, I wanted that message to spread like a virus and set free as many as would hear even a whisper of the greatness of our Savior.

The miracles don't happen in the boat. It is out on the waters where the Kingdom manifests. Our nets that were meant to fish for men will not fill up resting carefully inside boats. No, they need to be cast into the waters. The deeper the waters, the more the fish. Now, just think of the fishermen that cast the nets while he himself is out of the boat and on the water; what a great catch that would yield! Jesus has been searching for such people since the Testament of old, and He still was that day. There were over a hundred potential radical fishermen at that meeting, and I wanted to kick as many of them out of their comfortable boats as I could. The message felt incredibly anointed, but unfortunately it did not appear to produce the desired effect. It seemed more like a twig cast on a small fire giving rise to a bright but short lived flame only to become a smoldering coal on its way to becoming ash. Sad to say that would be the last time to date that I have been to the "corporate headquarters" of my old home church based fellowship. Following these events there appeared to be a chiasm forming, the aim of which was to separate me from the rest of the fellowship. This separation eventually led them to shun me and anyone that came to share with my ideologies. Baby Christians, even ones I had led to the Lord and prayed for to receive the Holy Spirit, were admonished to stay away from me. It took years for me to come to a place of forgiving them and having mercy on their mistakes while also coming to terms and recognizing my own.

Chapter 25: Back to Kansas

Following my trip to Kansas I remained in constant contact with Bo. It was only a few months later that I received an invitation to come out to a Christian conference their ministry was holding at a secluded resort in Kansas. They went on to tell me that there were evangelists from third world countries coming up to speak as well as a large group of local ministers. In fact, this conference was primarily for ministers. Finally, someone who actually believed I was a minister of the gospel. Actually, the truth is that all the people that I walked with before also could not deny God's call on my life, but when things got a little heated they retracted. I was a minister that came bearing a prophetic word or an anointed teaching that shattered present ways of thinking or living and a message that demanded change. Whenever this occurs the people that are not willing to change as the Lord leads them to, decide to demonize the messenger. This ploy has been going on since creation of man. Prophets in the Bible have been treated this way forever. In reality very few are actually willing to live for God. Pride, greed, self-righteousness and the love of money are but a few of the anchors that people are just not willing to release their boats from. Biblical Christianity has not changed: church has. I was always so confused looking at the state of most churches and observing not only their corporate behavior and lifestyle, but also that of those attending every Sunday morning service compared to the rest of their week. Sadly enough, most people seemed to be doing nothing more than putting on a good show. Dress up nice on Sundays; even carry around a Bible in a nice leather case. Sure they sang some songs with the worship team during the rehearsed set, and even threw a few dollars in the offering tray. Then of course, we must not forget the all-important handshake to greet the neighbors in adjacent pews. It all seemed so genuine at the time. But when the service ended, for most of the people there so did their Christianity for the week. But next Sunday morning the charade would start all over again. What God were they serving? The One I had met was all consuming. He was and is the great I AM! My days, my nights, and even my dreams were to become part of His Kingdom. After all, I tried building and managing my own kingdom for quite some time as does everyone else until they realize that all they are doing is signing up for a one way ticket to Hell. I would always ask (religious) self-professed Christians how their lives lined up with the saints in the Bible.

The repeated answer was:

"Well, that was for then...it is different now, and I do go to church."

I would get so irritated at the level of aloofness people showed in regards to the Lord. When did church substitute itself for God?! Where were the watchmen on the wall when this great atrocity happened? The very Greek word ecclesia, "church" in the Bible, is not a building or place to gather make-believe Christians in. No, it is actually supposed to be translated as: The called out ones to hear the voice of God. That's right, the church is supposed to be us! Us, the people that God created in His own image. Us, the people he died for and gave us the right to becomes sons of God. Us, who are blessed with the greatest privilege by allowing us to have the Holy Spirit dwell inside. How can you actually meet and walk with God and then act most of every day, week, and year like nothing changed? These questions have been the fuelling component of a zeal that has continually propelled me. My desire is to wake up the lethargic and aloof body of Christ to the realities of the Kingdom. There needs to be a spiritual earthquake at the epicenter of the church system. Altars need to be thrown down and the mercy seat and Jesus' throne need to be lifted high again. Let us return to the time when His people carried His presence before them in the great Ark of the Covenant, as we realize that we are the New Covenant Ark!

Back where we left off: Once I received the invitation from Bo to return to Kansas I was super excited. I went on immediately to share it with my wife, who shared in my excitement. We both just wanted to be anywhere the Lord was moving. The next thing I did was to share this with the two women that were still (kind of pretending to) mentor me. Their response was not the one I wished I had gotten. They rebuked me for even thinking about going, reminding me that I had financial debt, and that I would be in rebellion if I spent any money to go to Kansas. Again my spiritual balloon deflated in their presence. I just could not understand their way of thinking. What was I supposed to do owing so much? Was I supposed to get three jobs and work around the clock paying down as much of my debt as I could until I died or the Lord returned? What about the being a minister part of my life? Was that all meant to be second, third, or even fourth priority? Was I to leave the nets that Jesus gave me in the garage to collect dust? My mind and heart were in turmoil.

I did the smart thing and knelt down yet again. I remember that wonderful day clearly. I pleaded with God to speak to me about what I was to do. I could feel the spiritual oppression coming against me not to go. The persecution from my supposed fellowship was just as intense. I asked the Lord to please send someone to me to tell me if I was supposed to go. I told Him that if He did I would drop everything and go. You will never guess what happened: I was standing at the front desk of my chiropractic office talking about God to one of the receptionists. All of a sudden a man in his thirties came walking into the office. This was a man I had never met or talked to. He walked in very much like a man on a precise mission, you could see it in his eyes and in his demeanor. He walked right up to me and began to speak:

"The Lord says you are to go."

Wow! What an opening statement! But he was not finished yet:

"He also says not to listen to the voices rising up around you trying to stop you from doing His will."

Well, there you had it: time to pack. I was so grateful to God for all the times He had such mercy for me, speaking to me clearly whenever I did not know what to do. The man later on went on to share that he was shopping across the street at the local strip mall and that the Holy Spirit convicted him to come over and give me that message. I was so thankful for his obedience. I packed up shortly there-after and began another fourteen hour drive heading South-West.

This trip was much different than the last one. This time I had some idea as to why I was going, and I knew with certainty this was a God excursion. We arrived late that night and checked into a local hotel. My wife and I were so excited to be part of the Kingdom! We slept great that night preparing for a weekend with God and His people. After a quick breakfast the following morning we finished the last part of the trip ending at Tina's house to meet up with Bo. There we were again in that unassuming house where we had so freely worshipped together. The itinerary for the weekend was given to us and we were allocated a cabin to stay in on the retreat grounds. We began to catch up Bo and Tina as to what was going on back home in Michigan.

Shortly after we arrived a 25-year-old woman walked into the house. My "spider sense" went through the roof! I quickly looked at her and asked Bo who she was. He went on to tell me that she was a new convert to Tina's ministry and that they had all struggled with the fact she was demon possessed, and that up to that point they were unable to cast the demon out.

Well, there you go; just another day in the kingdom. When is the last time you have ever seen that conversation take place in the Baptist circuit or in most any other denominational American church? The answer is probably never. Now compare this story to the Bible. How often were demonized people coming to Jesus or the Apostles for deliverance? I rest my case. The underlining fact about this woman that made this situation even more uncomfortable was that she was six months pregnant. Bo went on to tell me that they had tried multiple times to cast it out but to no avail. He told me that if I felt led by the Lord to pray for her to cast it out to go ahead. I instantly asked God if he wanted me to, accepting the awesome opportunity to be part of such a great thing. His answer was that it was not yet time, a response I then relayed to Bo. The rest of the morning was spent helping them load up the vehicles in preparation for the retreat which was another hour or so drive from Tina's house.

The drive to the grounds where the retreat was scheduled was full of anxious anticipation for what God was going to do with us. As we arrived we were greeted by an elderly couple that seemed about as calm and peaceful as any I have ever met. We entered the large main building and immediately I knew that we were in a Godly facility. His presence and His peace saturated the building. It almost felt like we checked out of the world for that weekend. We helped everyone unload the vehicles, mostly the worship band's equipment. When the unloading was finished we were given keys to the cabin where Danielle and I were going to stay. The cabin was about 100 yards away down the side of a hill. We were then told to come back to the main building for dinner at 6 pm and that service would start about 8 pm.

My wife and I parked our car by the small cabin and unloaded our bags and suitcases. After this we walked around exploring a bit, and then returned to the cabin. We descended the small hill together holding hands. As we entered the small cabin we locked the door behind us. We were still very tired from the trip. My wife laid on the bed with a sigh now that she could finally relax for a bit. I began a quick exploration of the cabin amenities. It was in that very moment that the Holy Spirit spoke to me:

Craig Stasio

"Make love to your wife."

I was shell shocked! Did God really just talk to me about sex?! Did I really hear what I thought I did? Truth is, I was absolutely sure that I had heard exactly what He said. I quickly turned to my wife offering her a startled and confused stare, only to find her offering the same to me in return. I skittishly told her what I had heard. She with a startled face and a crackling voice said that she had just heard the same thing, too. We just could not understand how God wanted us to make love in that setting as soon as we arrived. We were on a God retreat weekend; we expected to pray, worship, be taught and teach, but sex was not on our mental spiritual itinerary. God though, for reasons unknown, had other plans. We yielded to His request and experienced one of the most beautiful sexual experiences we ever had. It started off very awkward because we both could feel the thick presence of God in the room with us. Although at first it felt weird, by the end it was awesome. God was bringing sexual healing to both of us, through each other, by his Spirit. In that moment He was teaching us the beauty of marital sexuality. Our entire sexual lives had been so polluted and perverted before knowing Jesus. God was now going to restore the fallen nature of our sexuality. From that day on the Lord has been very much a part of our lovemaking. We have even gotten to the point of speaking in tongues and worshiping during it. I know to some of you (if not most of you) this may stir you up a little or a lot, and that's okay; at first mention it stirred me, too. God came to restore all things, including sexuality (which He created by the way, not Satan). It was always meant to be a beautiful Godly experience to be shared in a marriage. My wife and I were finally learning this ourselves.

Chapter 26: Apprehending What You Were Apprehended For

Hours later dinnertime swept into the retreat site. We dressed for the night and proceeded up the hill again holding hands and feeling closer than we ever had. We quickly arrived in the onsite cafeteria style dining area. There were about one hundred guests attending this conference. Tables accommodating eight people each were spread around the large conference/dining room overlooking the Kansas hillsides. I was so hungry; I immediately went to the buffet lines to check out the fare. A Southern country flavor was what I witnessed. Foods that I normally did not eat were there awaiting me. I grabbed a plate and a fork and prepared to explore new foods. I grabbed two seats at Bo's table so that we could fellowship with him, not really knowing anyone else there. Not that I am at all uncomfortable sitting and mingling with strangers, to the contrary I love it. The meal was good, but the fellowship was great. We got to meet other ministers from South America and Africa. I must say it is so sad to hear about their testimonies and daily walks with the Lord and then compare them to the average Christian walk in North America. Nonetheless, I thoroughly enjoyed fellowshipping with them.

Dinner would eventually conclude and we were all ushered downstairs to a large worship area. The peace of God was saturating that room. The worship band began to play. I lost myself in the words and in my God. I was so grateful and privileged that God allowed me to be at that conference with these people of His. The worship was spontaneous and not a rehearsed set, allowing the Holy Spirit to move as he chose amongst us. The anointing on the songs was incredible. Tears began to stream down my face, as my arms lifted high to honor my Savior. The worship went on for close to an hour, after which a powerful prayer opened a door for the teaching to begin that evening.

The message that evening was: "Allow God to apprehend you for the work He apprehended you to do." In other words: Find out what He wants your life to be used for and do it! Perfect! A message right up my alley. The man taught with an incredible zeal and conviction. I was glued to my seat and to the message. The teaching or exhortation went on for about ninety minutes after which there was an altar call. This invitation to receive prayer was open to everyone in attendance. I was in! I was an Altar Call Specialist. Whenever a minister of the Lord offered to pray for me I was in the very front of the line. I could never get enough of God. I remember getting in the prayer line. I was about the fifth person in line. As he prepared to pray for people he shared that there were many people there that needed deliverance, and that the Lord would do exactly that. Well that sounded good to me. I was not sure what exactly I was going to get from God at the altar when he laid hands on me, but I did not care, I just wanted anything God was offering me. I watched as the first person was prayed for and their body started to shake like nothing I had ever seen to that point. All of a sudden they were keeled over on the ground and they were vomiting profusely. I could hear the evangelist screaming for the demons to come out from him. What a scene! I watched attentively as the next person in front of me went forward. The evangelist left the first person to the care of some of his staff and prepared to pray for the next person. A nervous anxiousness exploded inside me. What was going to happen to me when it was my turn?

"Maybe it was just that first person that was demonized," I thought, more so, hoped.

Well, I was about to find out because here came number two. It was not thirty seconds later that shouts of "Come out of her!" bellowed in that lower level room. There were now two people side by side on the carpet vomiting and curling up. It was time for a severe reality check. These were all ministers from around the world, some of which had been walking with the Lord for decades. I was astonished at the levels of demonic oppression and possession within these people. I realized that I was only two years old in the Lord, and if they were going through that after so many years, what was about to happen to me? I decided quickly that if there were demons like that in me I wanted them gone at any cost, even if I had to be a vomiting and riling public spectacle.

I then noticed that the woman directly in front of me was the demon possessed new member of Tina's ministry that Bo had told me about earlier that day. Boy, was I curious to see what happened when it was her turn. A curiosity that was satisfied no more than five minutes later. I watched her approach the evangelist and bow her head, closing her eyes. He approached her and laid his hands on her beginning to pray. The woman immediately started to violently shake and projectile vomit. The demon inside her also began to speak back at the evangelist, with a voice very much like the exorcist. Well, the Kingdom was happening right there in the middle of Kansas. Darkness and demons were getting vanquished. It was so exciting and exhilarating to watch all this, but now it was my turn. What a moment. You have to understand, there were two things I hated with all heart: flying and vomiting. And they were not always in that order. The thought of volunteering myself to experience the dreaded vomit experience was monumental to me. The motivating thought of returning home without any demons inside me outweighed the fear of vomiting. I braced myself and placed myself in front of the evangelist. My head bowed and my eyes closed preparing for whatever was to come. I told the Lord that I trusted Him, and to do whatever He had to; if there were demonic strongholds in me they needed to be purged. I could feel the evangelist approach as he was speaking in tongues under his breath. I could feel my body bracing itself for whatever the coming touch would result in. Finally, the anticipation and waiting would end as his rugged right hand pressed itself against my right shoulder.

While this all may sound crazy to you, and may appear to be over the top, put yourself in my shoes for a moment. There I was a semi-baby Christian, less than two years in the Lord and 800 miles away from home. The group I was with were ministers gathered from the four corners of the United States and third world countries. A view of the five people that were ahead of me in the prayer line all laid out on the floor writhing and vomiting with other assigned ministers of the head evangelist's group tending to and praying for them. Can you even imagine yourself in that setting? Let alone being the next person in line strapping yourself in for this spiritual roller coaster ride? If you can, then now you know where I was at emotionally.

Back to the potentially terrifying event: As the evangelist's hand touched me I felt a sense of peace come over me. I could feel that the Lord's presence around me and within me quicken. I was so relieved that the vomit session was not necessary for me. I just stood there peacefully and was prayed for. Unfortunately, I do not remember much of the prayer because I was so concerned and focused on potentially vomiting and having demons manifest in me. I will not say that I was disappointed in not being allowed to share the apparent corporate experience with those that went before me.

Now it was Danielle's turn, Round Two. Attentively, I watched her also go through the spiritual gauntlet preparing for the unknown. Glad to say that her experience was very close to mine: peace and comfort. The prayer line went on for over an hour. Besides the violent upheaving of demonic strongholds inside these ministers there was also another very common manifestation taking place. Almost all the people that were not vomiting were passing out seconds after hands being laid on them. I was not accustomed to seeing this happen, especially not so up close and personal. Some of the men that were a part of the evangelist's group would stand behind the people as they were about to get prayed for and ready themselves to catch a potentially falling Christian in front of them. I saw that Bo had rendered his services doing this. I looked over in his direction and his eyes captured my willing but curious look. He invited me to come join in with a simple and silent hand gesture. There I was standing behind my first potential falling Christian. I had never seen this in church. I was super attentive. I wanted to show them that I could be trusted to do this work. Truth be told I was so excited to be a part of something new that had anything to do with God. Well, ten seconds or so later the first one fell weightless into my arms. I could feel the state of absolute limpness their bodies as I softly lowered them to the floor, gathering and positioning myself for the next one. I now had become not only a fisher of men, but a catcher too. I was so encouraged to be trusted by God to do this. This process went on for the rest of the service. At the end of it all the scene looked something like this: People lying on the floor everywhere, some vomiting and manifesting demons that were trying to not be expelled, and others passed out in an apparent absolute peaceful bliss. Then there was me and my wife who had not been cast by the Lord into either of those categories. I remember very clearly the thoughts that began to run rampant in my mind.

"Why was I not vomiting or passed out?"

"Was there something wrong with me spiritually?"

"Was God in some way disappointed in me? And if so how could I get it right so that I to could get the full experience here with the rest of them."

I will tell you that in the next year or so I attended countless conferences and meetings like this one all over the world; and the same thing happened to me every time. I had not started to vomit or be exposed to any apparent exorcism related event. Also, I never was subjected to passing out under the manifestation of the Holy Spirit as ministers prayed for me. There were times that I was in a prayer line of close to a hundred people and at the end of all the prayers I would be the only one standing. I must tell you the repeated incidents took a toll on me emotionally. I did not want to be excluded from anything in my Father's Kingdom. There was a part of me that was getting very scared on the inside about all this.

I finally got real with God and asked Him to please tell me why this was happening to me. The request happened on my knees with worried and sincere tears flowing down my face. I knew that my always faithful God had heard and was already in the process of answering. I rose from the floor and prepared to go about my day as a fisher of men. That very special day someone came up to me holding a book from a well-known prophet from North Carolina. They had just read a passage from one of the chapters and felt very strongly that the Lord wanted them to share with me what they had just read. I excitedly invited them to please proceed. This portion of the chapter talked about a coming time where the Lord wanted His people to not fall under the anointing of His Holy Spirit, but to stand so that He could use them to minister. Wow! What a great message for me to hear! How wonderful was that little spiritual nugget?! That simple event brought so much peace and clarity to me that it was priceless.

Well, back to the conference, day two. The night before we had an incredibly peaceful night of sleep. My wife did share with me that she had felt something like electricity flowing through her body all night from being prayed for. We awoke at about 8 am and got ready for 9 am breakfast at the cafeteria. As we arrived most of the other guests were already there and most of them appeared to be engaged in deep spiritual conversations and small group prayers. It was so awesome to see other people that took the Kingdom life seriously. I sat at the same table as Bo again and we talked about the previous night. I found it so ironic that the people that ran the facility had told us to please not bring any food or drink other than bottled water into the area where the services were held. They informed us that they had just changed all the carpet down in that area and wanted to try and preserve its new state as long as possible. The ironic part is that we did honor their request, but that all seemed to be in vain due to all the vomiting. Bo went on also to tell me that there were some people still going through deliverance after my wife and I left until close to 3 am. Again, I can't emphasize how different this all was from any church service we had ever attended back home in Michigan.

The next day of this new process was now underway; we began by having another service after breakfast. This event was very similar to the last one. People gathered in a prayer line after the message. Again, I was in the front portion of the line. I wondered what would happen this time now that all those demons had been cast out the night before. It did not take long at all to get that answer. The first woman bowed her head and the evangelist again placed his hand on her as he began to pray for her. Guess what happened next? Yep, more vomit.

"Here we go again," I thought.

I hoped desperately that I would again escape this component of the getaway. Eventually it became my turn and I closed my eyes, bowing my head in anticipation. As before, all I felt was peace, no vomiting, and no passing out. Immediately after I was prayed for, Bo came to get me and asked me if I would not mind "catching" again. What a weird thing for me. But I guess that was the best way to get close to the action. I got to be within inches of the people as the evangelist laid his hands on them. I got to feel the presence of God splash against them, sometimes like soft soothing waves of comfort, other times like tidal waves of deliverance. Either way I wanted to get as spiritually wet as possible. Not to mention I wanted to try and figure out how the whole passing out thing worked. The line would eventually all get prayed for and ministered to and there they were again. A great mass of humanity laying on the floor in a large clump. Some vomiting and purging some of the most demonic sounds from their mouths as demons were expelled, others apparently in a state of rest and peace, almost asleep. And again let's not forget about me, standing over all these people looking down wondering why I was not on that floor, too.

Chapter 27: Lessons in Exorcisms

I was particularly fascinated with watching a very specific individual there. This was a large man that the night before seemed by far to have the most intense episodes of deliverance I had ever seen. He was the last one to leave the night before according to Bo. Here he was this afternoon in the same state as the previous night; I watched him vomiting and curled up on the floor like he was being zapped with intense electricity. The head evangelist and some of his core staff were all kneeled over him. I could see a fiery look in the evangelist's eyes as he intensely stared at the man and yelled over and over: 'Come out of him in Jesus' name!" What a sight! I went closer and watched. I wanted to learn as much as I could about this whole "casting out demons" thing from them as I could. I did have some experiences back home doing this when I preached to people and then prayed for them. But, I still thought, you can never know too much about this subject.

I remembered reading a story in the Book of Acts where seven sons of a Jewish priest name Sceva came across a demon possessed man. They had all witnessed Paul (formerly known to them as Saul of Tarsus) casting demons out of such people. They decided to take their shot at doing it, too. The result: the demon took all seven of them and beat them close to death. They were barely able to get away alive (and naked). The part of the story that seemed to imbed itself in my mind was what the demon said to them as they first approached the possessed man. The men had commanded the demon: "In the Name of the Jesus that Paul preaches we command you to come out of this man."

I guess they obviously though this would work. They assumed that the ingredients to a successful exorcism was the eloquence of the statements given, demanding the evil presence vacate the human vessel. Or perhaps it was their Jewish bloodline, after all, they were sons of a priest. This is how the demon inside the man responded:

"Jesus we know...and Paul we have heard of. But, who are you?"

What a meaty statement:

"Jesus we know."

That made sense to me. He is God, the Creator of all things, even of the beings that later became demons. That part was simple and to the point for me. It was the next part that captured so much more of my attention: "Paul we have heard of."

Wow! That meant demons actually talked to each other about the men and woman of God. It was clear to me from this statement that there must had been other demons that had actually encountered this converted Saul that had now became a powerful messenger of Jesus named Paul. It was also apparent to me that when these demons came across Paul that they must have had quite a memorable encounter, probably resulting in them being evicted from their human host. This magnified the reality that the power inside of Paul was far more powerful than the demons'. Then came the last part of the statement:

"But, who are you?"

To me this portion seemed to relay the absolute level of irrelevance these men meant to the demonic creatures inhabiting the possessed man. Those seven men were no more significant to those demons and that event than a small group of ants strolling at our feet. I noticed that they had used Jesus' name, but that did not seem to have any effect on. So there was obviously some missing ingredient. All I knew when I first read that story in scripture is that I wanted with all my heart to be like Paul. I wanted demons to know of me, the man of God named Craig, that had the power of the Kingdom within him and on his side. I actually prayed to God immediately after reading that story that He would allow me to become a man like that. A request I now know the Lord has granted as I walk as a nine and a half-year-old minister of the Lord to date.

But, back to the story: I was being allowed to watch a tremendous event up close as the power of God expelled these nasty creatures from within the people that were so oppressed by them. I did not quite understand the vomiting part accompanying the expulsion, but that was okay; I just wanted to learn as much as I could. It later dawned on me that the reason the seven sons of Sceva were unable to influence the state of that demon is that they were exactly what they were called: sons of Sceva, not sons of God. There had to be an actual adoption in the Spirit before you had legal spiritual right to impose the authority of Jesus' name. In other words: you needed to be born again. Such a simple concept when you really think about it. But still a concept that has evaded so many in the present day "church system".

It troubles me deeply to know the amount of people attending services week after week and year after year, never having been born again. Thinking that their service and sacrifice of Sunday morning time will somehow merit them access into the great Kingdom of our God. Not understanding that being born again is not a natural event that occurs from saying a few scripted words at an altar but that it is a supernatural event that can only occur at the drawing and leading of the Holy Spirit. It is an act of grace; unmerited and undeserved. A true conversion is the result of a state of brokenness brought on by the conviction of the Holy Spirit. The person is brought to a deep internal knowledge of their own depravity. The remorse to follow for such a state of existence can then lead one to cry out for mercy to the only one able to grant it: JESUS! Following these steps the person will then experience the heavenly gift: being born again, the first in many steps to eventually inheriting salvation.

Craig Stasio

Unfortunately, so many in the church have been deceived and lulled to spiritual sleep thinking that they are born again, sons of the King, when no such thing has ever really occurred. So many of the parables Jesus taught exemplified this very scary reality. The one that stands out the most to me is when He had his wedding banquet and the guests were all present. Jesus then saw a man there that did not have the proper attire. He turned to ask that man:

"Friend, how did you get in here dressed like that?"

"Friend", what an opening. That He did not use the word "son" said it all to me. There is no comparison between the emotional, spiritual, and natural bond of a friend versus a son. It was already apparent to me when reading this parable that the man was not born again. The conclusion of Jesus' first statement laid out the reality that this man did not have the proper attire to be there: the robe of righteousness, something that you get once you are born again. Nope, he was just another man that had been at functions of the King. He had eaten from His table and been in His presence and that of His people, but never been born again and really and truly become His. After this question Jesus has him extracted violently from this banquet and bound in the presence of the other guests present. The conclusion of the parable: this unwanted guest (an imposter) is cast into Hell for all eternity. The most horrifying and sad reality to me reading that parable is that he could have received the robe and been allowed access to that glorious banquet had he just done it God's way: humbled himself to be born again. I have pondered in distress so many times how many "church people" are going to end up at that banquet with the wrong attire. That is why I try to share the zealous and life-saving message of John 3:6:

"You must be born again to enter His Kingdom!"

Well, as I was saying before: I watched this man going through some of the most physically and emotionally demanding deliverance I had ever seen in my walk up to that point. He was squirming like a piece of bacon in the frying pan, emitting horrifying sounds and screams. The evangelist was unaffected by this rampant manifestation of demonic nature. Eventually, after about 45 minutes of intense deliverance, the evangelists walked away from the man that was still on the floor. His appearance was not that of a man that had actually been delivered. Nope, there was obviously still substantial work that needed to be done. But, for whatever reason, that work would not take place now. My eyes then shifted to the evangelist. I could see a level of apparent exhaustion in his face and his eyes. The man had just fought a tremendous battle and I could tell that he needed some sort of a spiritual reprieve and re-charging. I then looked around to see if my wife was still there or if she had gone back to the cabin to wait for me. To my pleasant surprise she was still there peacefully and quietly praying in one of the chairs by herself. I went to gather her and we went back to our room for some rest. We also were able to process together all that had happened up to that point. It was so wonderful to have a soul mate to walk with that you can share all things with. I was so blessed to have this wife that the Lord prompted me to marry!

It did not take long for dinnertime to come. My wife and I had spent a short time napping after the last service. There we were again gathered with the large group of excited ministers in the cafeteria. I was encouraged to see the level of joy radiating from everyone (even all the people that had just been vomiting hours before). This truly was an awesome gathering event of the Body of Christ. More fellowship was shared over a simple meal leading up to the nightly service. As the previous two, that night's service was almost an exact replica of the two before it. An incredible message, followed by an invitation to prayer. This time felt a little different for me though, and I mean that in a good way. Sure, I figured I would become a catcher again as soon as they were done praying for me (provided I was able to avoid a bout of vomiting and spiritually induced unconsciousness). Still, I felt that there was something special for me that evening. This was all confirmed when it became my turn to receive prayer and not only did the evangelist pray for me again, but the host of the conference also joined in and laid hands on me as well. The woman then began to prophesy some really awesome things over me, things that blew me out, so to speak. (Don't worry, I will let you know about them at a later time when it will make more sense to you.) Suffice it to say, I felt that those prophetic words would begin to shape my spiritual future; to begin chiseling the man I was, on the way to producing the one I was going to become. The night would end as the one before it: people on the floor, and you know the rest. And as at every other meeting: that one demonized man going through insane deliverance off in a corner. I had found it interesting that at every meeting that one very demonized man was always seated between the evangelist and the leader of the conference in the front row. I wondered if that was an act of protection for the rest of us, because at that time nothing else made sense. But I would get my answer the next day.

Chapter 28: Communion and The Fear of the Lord

Saturday morning exploded with bright rays of sunshine on those little hillsides in the middle of Kansas. We had no problem waking up that morning. We were both excited to see what the culmination of this conference was going to look like. We had felt a spiritual crescendo happen from service to service, and felt that today's services would not disappoint. Eggs, bacon, and toast were allowed their half hour of attention, and off to fellowship we went. The pre-service fellowship had now evolved into people actually ministering to each other and praying for each other. This was very encouraging for my wife and I. We had longed for fellowship like this since the beginning of our walks. 11:00 am service came quickly. To our surprise, though, there would be no morning service. Instead, the leadership had decided to break us into small groups for something called a foot washing. Now, I know that the name itself states a lot about the event. Regardless, I was still very curious and nervous about the whole thing. I did not know if it entailed giving, receiving, or both. I was somewhat uncomfortable thinking of a group of men in a small room washing my feet. That said, I felt like this foot washing was prompted by the Lord, so I yielded and agreed to the process.

We were placed into groups of five or six people and then led to individual rooms and given a large basin with warm water, buckets, and towels. Each of us were also told to make sure to bring our Bibles along. We were then instructed to take turns washing each other's feet. And, if during this process we heard anything from the Lord for the person we were encouraged to share it with them. In reality, the set-up was more of one where you were expected to hear something for the person. As each person was having their feet washed we would go around the circle of people in the room and wait in silence until they spoke something. Most people read Scripture to the person. Others gave words of encouragement. There were some that went as far as to prophesy over them. It was here that I learned my now commonly used slang slogan; because it was here that the reality was birthed for me. The phrase I am speaking of describes what came from others as they tried to mimic the real prophetic gift flowing in the room. That word is "prophe-lying". It was my way to express verbal statements given under the guise of being prophetic words, but originating from people's own imaginations and/or souls. These false prophetic words seemed to be a potential for serious spiritual damage to the individual receiving the message. People would hang onto these words to the point of changing their lives to line up with those words at any cost. I learned early in my walk that all the changing and directed shifts in my life and that of my wife would occur at the hand of the Lord. There was little to no effort at all on my part to make such words and promises come to pass, other than timely obedience to the leadings of the Holy Spirit. Those powerful prophetic words given to me through my walk have all been more of a confirmatory word to a future event or state that I would find myself in. All this said, the washings went on with all the accompanying manifestations, including "prophe-lying". This session would go on for about two hours for our group of six men. As we exited the small room together we felt bonded together in the Spirit, a special kinship of sorts. We then realized that it was already time for lunch.

Like a hungered pack of wolves we made a beeline to the buffet. As I started eating I could see that my wife was not there yet. She had been sent into another room, and five other women with her. I was surprised that they were still going at it; after all, we had been quite thorough in our session. As I looked into the room where she was I could see that they were very much still in the process. I was a little sad, because I wanted to eat lunch with my wife. I managed to find Bo again and sit with him at his table. I was then blessed to have the main preaching evangelist come and sit by me at our table. I took this opportunity to pick his brain as much as I could. We had some incredible dialogue and fellowship. He shared wild stories of his life and his ministry back home in South America, and I shared some of mine as well. We hit it off very nicely. The man even gave me his number and told me that if I ever felt led to have a conference in Michigan he would come and speak. After about another hour I noticed that my wife had still not been released from her foot bathing event. I expressed my concern about that to Bo and he went off to examine the situation. The people at the lunch area were already packing up the food, and I wanted to make sure my wife got what she wanted to eat for lunch before it was all gone. Shortly there-after my wife joined us and prepared herself an adequate lunch from what remained available. She went on to tell me that she wanted to escape from her predicament, but she felt like she could not until they were all done. She also had had the wonderful (I say that sarcastically) experience of witnessing profuse "prophe-lying", it appeared even more than I had. She was disappointed at the level of carnal and soulish words given mixed in with the real prophetic. We both felt that this had a tremendous spiritual diluting effect on the hearers. But there was nothing we could do about it now.

Another brief nap was needed in preparation for what we hoped would be the grand finale. We were both prepared to be up as late as needed to get all we could out of this all important session. We awoke in a state of severe excitement at about 5:30 pm, with just enough time to shower and get ready for dinner. We were again gathered with the flock at dining tables with freshly prepared tacos and taco salads. The time was finally upon us: seven o' clock. In a single file we entered the service room. There seemed to be much more of a seriousness about this event than all the others. Danielle and I sat in the fifth row to the right of the stage. The worship began. The intensity this time was far greater than any of the other worship sessions leading up to the teachings. I knew something big was going to happen that night. The worship would eventually yield to a corporate prayer led by the conference director, and this is where it all got really crazy!

The woman began to pray one of the most powerful prayers I had ever heard, and then she addressed the crowd. She went on to tell us that we were about to partake in communion. And that we needed to seriously reflect upon the finished work of the Lord at the Cross, and our dedication to his cause. She then said a sentence that I will never forget:

"I am now going to ask our Father to come as we take communion."

This perked my ears. She then bowed her head and did exactly that. My wife and I had already been given a small paper cup of juice and a wafer of sorts. I was there holding each with one hand. I had taken communion in church before, and although some of those events were wild, this one would top them all to date. Immediately, and I mean immediately, a thick and undeniable presence of God filled that room. I began to shake on the inside from my core. Not only that, but my body was now doing the same.

Astonished and somewhat overcome by the event I quickly looked over at my wife. Danielle was found in a similar state shaking and crying. I did not know what to do. The emotions only intensified as the presence of the Lord grew each passing second. Normally in that situation I would turn into the protective, encouraging husband for my spouse. But on that night I was so undone that I could not have been of help to her. My shaking was increased to an apparent state of complete systemic shock. I could not stop what was happening to me. I really wish I could take you through this next portion of the event second by second, as so much of the details escape me, but I will though, tell you all that I do recall. Keep in mind now, that I was quite the old school man and husband. Meat and potatoes when it came to showing external manifestations of internal emotional struggles. I don't exactly know how I ended up where I did, but I found myself under a small table off to the side shaking and crying frantically. I remembered vaguely looking over and seeing my wife in a similar state off on the other side of the room by herself. Then I also noted everyone there in a similar state.

There was a presence of God there that struck you with fear to your core. I had read about the Fear of the Lord plenty. I had also had multiple experiences where the Holy Spirit manifested to me and through me in that format, but never like this! I was undone! I did not know what to do, so I sat there crying and thanking Him for the cross and all His sacrifice to save wretched me. I also told Him that I did want to serve Him and follow Him with my life. The childlike moment I had with the Lord at that time was priceless. I looked attentively at the juice and the wafer in my hands as I wiped away the tears with my sleeve. I did not really understand what was going on, but I knew that partaking in this communion was different in the greatest of wonderful ways. I slowly ate the wafer prepared for about anything to happen. Then the juice followed. My mind reflected intensely on the Cross, but now even more on the glorious throne in Heaven where Jesus sits and rules. I could feel His kingship and authority in that moment. I knew beyond any doubt that He was second to none! As I was reflecting and almost caught in a vision of all this the conference director escorted a man to the pulpit. I knew it was quite strange for a teaching to now come while we were all on the floor crying and shaking. But yet, here was how the meeting would go next:

As my eyes focused through the tears I could now see clearly the man that was being given the pulpit to speak from on this ever powerful final session of the conference. To my astonishment it was the demonized man that had spent the better part of two and a half days shaking like bacon on the floor through hours and hours of demonic deliverance. It was here that humility grabbed hold of me like a vice. It would have been very easy to discard the words to come from that vessel if I had not spiritually discerned the moment. In that moment I remembered the scripture about not discerning anyone according to the flesh but by the Spirit. And that is exactly what I did. I could absolutely tell that that man was anointed to give whatever message was about to come forth from his mouth. Even though I felt uncomfortable there on the floor I knew I could not move if I wanted to, I was still frozen by the Fear of the Lord. The man began to share what it was like for the past sixty or so hours. He went on to tell us that he was a pastor from Kentucky, and that he was the biological brother of the woman hosting the conference. The story unfolded as he told us of his recent bout of rebellion. And how he had run away from his call and his spiritual responsibilities in the Kingdom to indulge in the things of the world. For some time his sister had been trying to minister to him over the phone, and she had even traveled to see him to try and offer help. Finally, the Lord had gotten through to him enough to get him to come to this conference. The high level of deliverance was the means the Lord used to bring about spiritual restoration to this vessel of His. After all this, there he was, the one entrusted with the most powerful anointing and message of the entire conference. This night taught me to never doubt in the absolute restorative power of the Lord. And, that He can truly make all things new with every touch of His Spirit!

The message given by this mighty man of God was an invitation to be used mightily by the Lord in the years to come. The criteria for acceptance was understanding that it would cost you everything: even your own life. This was an answer to so many of my tear filled prayers. I had pleaded with the Lord alone in my prayer time to use my life and death for His glory. The man instructed us all to weigh the cost before daring to come up to that pulpit to receive the anointing and impartation of such a great commissioning. Close to twenty minutes transpired as we all stood, or should I say laid, on the floor and meditated on what he said. For me it was not much of a choice, I would have rather just died than not follow my call in His Kingdom. There was nothing I desired more. Reality though, I was being called to actually lay my life on that altar. And everything that was part of my life for the Lord to do with as He pleased. I felt very much like Abraham leading his precious son Isaac up the mountain to that altar. The Fear of the Lord on me only intensified, close to paralyzing me. It was then that I noticed the first people daring to make their way up to that pulpit. The man stopped them and told them to go back to where they were. And that they had not taken his message as seriously as they should have. He emphasized the "everything" that God was requiring. And that they were going to be asked to sign a blank contract before and with the Lord. A contract that He will then fill out at His good pleasure, regardless of the price He would then ask us to pay. I could see the level of serious contemplation now engulf the people that had prematurely approached. After a short period of time another small group of people began to walk up again. I was still frozen on the floor unable to move, crying and shaking, caught up in the majesty of my King. The man again stopped them and gave an even sterner version of the rebuke he had given the group that went before them. The presence of the Lord exploded in that place. I had a small taste of Isaiah's experience when he was before the Lord. I felt undone, like a dead man. The second group of people too, where shooed back to their seats to reflect on what the Lord was asking, or better yet, demanding, of those that would choose to come forth and accept this holy invitation. Another ten to twenty minutes elapsed before the altar was actually opened for the willing. I cried out to the Lord to get me on that alter at any cost. I could not actually get my legs to respond, and I mean that very literally. I could try and walk you through laws of physics and of human kinesiology and biomechanical neuromuscular physiology as to why this was possibly happening. Truth be told I knew the reason was that the Lord had pinned me to that floor. The same way when His presence fell at King Solomon's dedication of the temple: all the priests bit the dust. Well this priest from Michigan was no different in that regard, I had thoroughly bit the dust that evening. To feel such a tangible and physical manifestation of the Holy Spirit was exhilarating. I wish that everyone could be exposed to such an encounter, I am sure that it would extinguish unbelief faster than carbon dioxide foam extinguishes a flame. But then again, that encounter was not an instance to produce faith, but an encounter resulting from faith. I started to talk out loud to emphasize my desperate desire to reach that altar. Asking in my mind was not enough for me anymore. The people around me heard my desperate pleas to the Father. I begged Him to send an angel to carry me forward if my body was not going to be allowed to do so on its own. My prayer was answered as my body's faculties returned to being mine to command. I rose cautiously and with a level of seriousness that I do not think I had ever had before about anything. I made my way to the altar and was the fourth person to do so. I took a position of kneeling on the floor, one that quickly resulted in me lying prostrate on the floor in tears and awe. I could see the man preparing to lay hands and pray for those that had come forth, including me. I watched the first girl in line preparing for this. She was the older daughter of the woman that led the conference. I watched the event unfold, and as it did the fear of the Lord consumed me. I witnessed the man lay hands on the girl and she violently vomited and started to scream and dry heave. This was all so scary. But I knew this was the Lord so I did not completely lose heart. My prayer at that moment was one that now I laugh about profusely, but believe me it was very genuine and not funny at all back then: I asked the Lord to please not let me pee on the floor where anyone else may get wet by it. The prayer came as a result of me feeling like I actually was going to pee myself. I watched the second girl get prayed for and again the same result happened. Well I thought that this time there was not going to be any escaping for me. The all-dreaded vomiting might actually happen to me. In reality, as much as I hated vomiting, I was so concerned and engulfed in the rest of what was happening that I just didn't care. Now, the third person to the altar's turn. To this one I just closed my eyes as she was right next to me also prostrate on the floor. I felt like a child in a small bathroom hearing the roaring of an impending tornado about to ravage the house, closing my eyes and bracing myself for the spiritual impact.

I could feel the man approach me. I could almost smell the odor of his shoes by my face. The time was upon me. I completely yielded my body, mind, soul, and spirit to the Lord. The minister's large and powerful hand laid itself against my back. I could feel the anointing penetrate me, but no vomiting and no writhing. I opened my eyes to see that I had not peed myself and that all was okay. I laid there thanking the Lord for everything in tears. Caught up in the wonder of Him allowing someone like me the privilege of being used for such a cause. I arose to a standing position and returned quietly to join my wife who had now made her way back to her initial chair. I sat next to her and held her. I did not know what to say, I was way too blown out by the whole event. I did not need to help catch anyone that night because the ones that came forward already started on their face. We eventually returned to the cabin and laid there so grateful to have been invited there. We finally got to sleep at about 3 am.

Chapter 29: Breaking Free of Witchcraft

I was suddenly awoken at about 8:15 am I knew that it was God waking me up. I quickly asked Him what He wanted me to do. I could feel His tangible presence in the room. He directed me to go open the cabin door. What an exhilarating moment, it was almost like seeing you had a delivery package from UPS arrive not knowing what was in it. The fact that I had only slept for a brief period that night had me a little groggy but still very responsive to this unction of God's. I could see my hand turning the knob as I prepared yet again for My Father to invade my life in ways only He could do. The smell of the brisk morning dew outside captivated my senses and the cooler temperatures clashed with the preset warmth of our room. My eyes then focused to see if I could ascertain the reason for me being driven to do this. Right in front of me not more than five feet away I could see the back of a flannel shirt on a reasonably large man that appeared to be walking away from my cabin. I had no idea who he was or why he was there that morning. The thick presence of God reassured me that I did not need to know such things in order to trust that it was okay, and that we were safe. Not knowing whether he had heard me open the door or not I bellowed out a simple but excited "Good morning." I could see the sound of my voice capture his attention. His step away from the cabin ceased as he appeared to pause, almost as if caught in a deep state of internal reflection. Not more than a few seconds later he turned in my direction and stared right at me. There he was, a man in his sixties. The age was given away by the greyish tone of his hair and the years of life painted across the features of his face. I could see without any doubt that the man was processing something attentively in his mind. I could see a state of turmoil gripping him in the midst of his own silence. Anxiously I awaited some verbal clue as to his presence there in the middle of the woods that morning at my cabin door. Eventually his thoughts would become sound, and a shaking voice began to emit the first of many sentences I would come to hear from this stranger.

"I told God I did not want to come here."

Well that was definitely a classic opening to my new life's initial dialogue with a stranger. I quickly reflected on two parts of that opening statement. The first part was that he did not want to be there. That portion of the statement had me a little concerned. I wondered why he did not want to come. More importantly what was he sent to do? Were his reservations about carrying out the task assigned to him founded on the instructions given him, or were they centered around me? All this intrinsic meditation came to a peaceful halt as I then recalled the most important part of that opening statement; "God." That's right, God had sent him. I knew instantly that this was a very important encounter. God had awakened me from a deep sleep to open the door. The stringent push to awaken me so abruptly to do this now made sense in lieu of me having just witnessed this stranger attempting to quietly walk away from our cabin unnoticed. I knew God did not want me to miss out on whatever was meant to take place there that wonderful morning. It was in that moment that it dawned on me, I had just signed the blank contract with God the night before. A rapid state of panic and fear began a takeover attempt on my soul, as my thoughts ran wild:

"Was this man here to take me away to die as a martyr?"

"Was God about to have me walk away from everything and everyone as a test of my recent commitment of faith?"

These thoughts ravaged my being in the seconds to follow.

I felt like a Marine awoken in the barracks only to see the silhouette of my Sargent standing there with a recently opened letter in his hand, and a perplexed and worried look on his face. Knowing that he was about to give us a directive passed down to him from the chain of command. An order that apparently had given him pause and concern. Yes that is exactly what I felt like. And the Marine analogy is perfectly fitting. After all I was taught early in my walk that God's Kingdom is very much like the military. He is the great general of His army, the Lord of Hosts. There are multiple ranks in this prestigious army of His. I knew that the previous night I had signed up to be a special operations soldier. I had agreed by going to that alter to give away all aspects of my life to my general, my King. The fact that a strange man was now at my cabin door bearing His name could be nothing more than a response to my recent actions. Surely he was there with a directive from above, one that he appeared to not want to carry out. It dawned on me then that maybe he felt bad for me. And that he did not want to relay the given instructions concerning my life. Maybe he was even scared for me. What a life I live. I am sitting at my computer writing this passage of my story with a smile giving way to a simple laugh as I recall those early days on my Christian walk. Well, back to the story:

Wanting some sort of closure about why he was there I began to walk towards him and offered a simple handshake of friendship. "Hi, my name is Craig, I know God sent you here." I figured it would be good to reassure him that he was actually there sent by God, and not on his own accord. I paused for a brief moment to allow enough silence for him to speak. He gazed right at me and finally began to talk. He explained to me that the Lord had been talking to him about my wife and I for a few days. He also shared with us that he was sent there to help us. It was in that moment that the Holy Spirit spoke softly to me to go and get my wife and bring her into this adventure. I walked to the bedroom to get her, inviting this man in and asking him to wait for me in the small foyer. This morning encounter now included Danielle as well. She was nervous as I escorted her to the entrance of the cabin to introduce her to the strange man. I then realized that I had not even heard his name yet, just that he was a reluctant man sent by God to help us.

The Holy Spirit within me prompted me to send my wife to talk to him alone. My immediate obedience to this startled both my wife and the man. They were surprised that I would allow my beautiful bride to be alone with this strange man without any apparent concern for her safety. In reality I am a very protective man when it comes to my wife. But how could I worry about her when I knew that she was in the strong hands of my Father, her Father. I watched the two of them walk about 25 feet down the cabin's long porch. They then stopped and a simple dialogue began to unfold. I could see my wife look back from time to time and see if I was still there, my attention and presence made her feel safe enough to be in this situation. The two of them exchanged a conversation that could not have lasted more than ten minutes and they both walked back towards me. I had spent those minutes praying and thanking God for allowing me the tremendous opportunity to be part of this retreat and of the all-important alter call from the previous night. I also thanked Him for sending this man to offer us some sort of needed help. The long arms of my Father's love had reached out to me way out there in a cabin in the middle of Kansas.

The rugged terrain of my recent relationships had brought about severe wear and tear on my heart. Back in Michigan there was no longer a natural venue of emotional support for me and Danielle. Our fellowship was deeply entrenched in a hostile stance in my regards. Most everyone thought I had lost my mind. My emotional tank was running close to empty. What a fill-up this weekend had offered me. My tank was again saturated with love and encouragement. Although almost all the attacks were centered around and directed at me, I knew they had taken an immense toll of my spouse. I wanted to help her in any way I could, and if that man was the answer then I was all for it. So many times I felt helpless watching my wife go through intense emotional situations leading to tears and pain. Her pain pierced my heart more than my own. I prayed to God so many times to protect and help that woman I so love. This for sure was a great answer to all those heart felt petitions to His Throne.

As the two of them reached the area where I was sitting they began to speak. I was informed that the man's name was Dave, and that he was a minister for thirty or so years. He shared that God had given him a specific directive to come and help me and Danielle. He then asked me if he could pray for her, explaining that she needed some deliverance. Flash backs from the previous three days of people vomiting and writhing on the floor filled my mind instantly. But all these fear eliciting memories were brushed away by the desire for Danielle to receive whatever freedom the Lord was offering her through Dave. My answer was a yes, of course. I watched this tentative man place his hands on my wife's shoulder and began to pray. I could feel the authority in his humble voice as he began to request help from our Father. He then began to share a vision of what he was seeing to us. He said that the Lord had showed him an image of two women. He went on to describe their rough age and physical appearances as he was seeing them. He continued on by sharing with us that the Lord was showing him that they had taken their positions of authority in our lives and had operated in a spirit of witchcraft over us, especially Danielle. He went on to say that he could see spiritual hooks of this witchcraft implanted in my wife's back with cords or chains coming from these two women. And it was then that I witnessed one of the first profound prophetic acts in my walk. Dave raised his right hand configuring his fingers in a way as if preparing to break a set of layered bricks with a karate chop. He then rapidly appeared to strike at the invisible spiritual cords protruding from her back while he loudly shouted out:

"I break these hooks of witchcraft over Danielle in Jesus' Name!"

Witchcraft! You can only imagine of where that word led my mind to. The description of the two woman was a carbon copy of the two ladies that had been mentoring us back in Michigan. I had watched our relationships systematically deteriorate, but witchcraft?! Truth be told, I did not really have a good understanding at that time as to what the word actually implied. As most other people the word brought immediate visons to my mind of old women riding broomsticks and black cats. But now with the little knowledge and experience I had received in my infantile level of training up to that time I had a slightly better picture. I knew of the reality of real witches and covens. I was quite aware of their servitude to demonic forces and, and their pacts to worship Satan. I had already encountered and been confronted by more than one. Encounters that empirically proved the spiritual reality that my God was and will always be greater than theirs!

I watched as my wife almost keeled over caught up in an apparent emotional catastrophe. She began to not only hyperventilate, but tears began to violently cascade down her face. It all reminded me of what happens when a human body rejects an organ transplant. There is a violent attempt by the receiving body's immune system to destroy the foreign organ. The same thing appeared to be happening here in the spirit. I could see her being set free from whatever curses had been spoken over her from these two women. That's right, I said curses. I am sure to most of you that all sounds really weird and potentially crazy. But trust me that is exactly what had occurred. They had actually cursed my wife. At the time I really had a limited understanding of the principles of curses and blessings. Let it suffice to say that I still knew it was all very real and very important. Curses are verbally unleashed statements that are spoken against the person being affected. As believers, especially Holy Spirit filled believers we have tremendous power behind the words we speak.

In the Book of James it talks about how the believer has the ability to either curse or bless someone with their tongue. There I was in the middle of a situation that proved the reality of this principle. I watched my wife experience some of the most intense deliverance I ever had on the patio of that distant cabin. The whole experience lasted about fifteen minutes. I felt so helpless, but at the same time I felt absolutely assured that she was okay. After all she was in our Father's hands. What better place than that could she ever be? I was so touched by the level of love and attentiveness that God showed my wife by sending this man to her aid. Of course I then also began to ponder if he had been sent only for my wife, or was he also sent on some sort of mission regarding me. Well, as the whole process with my wife seemed to come to a favorable conclusion, I prepared to get my answer.

Dave migrated quietly in my direction. I was still sitting on the rugged bench located by the foyer of the building. I looked up at him advancing towards me. In the few seconds available prior to this apparent spiritual impact I tried to discern what was coming. I had two things to go on. The first was that my God and Father were good. And I mean absolutely good. There was no evil in Him. All He wanted for me was the best. Therefore I always knew that His gestures in my regards were restorative and edifying. The second thing that gave me comfort was the fact I had just watched my wife receive a level of spiritual freedom at the hands of this stranger. Dave slowly lowered his body to sit right next to me on the bench. I could see that it was not only me trying to analyze the other person. Dave was intently trying to see what I was all about, I could feel the probative nature in his silent stare. It was in the absolutely awkward silence that the most beautiful thing happened: I could hear a subtle but healthy laugh coming from the soft voice of God inside me. This was a first for me. I had never really heard God laugh before, and definitely not like that. I was somewhat caught up in the potential reality of God ravaging my life in a whole new way now that I had given him carte blanche over my life the night before. I had prepared my pounding heart for just about anything possible in those mere seconds preceding the coming dialogue with Dave, a messenger from our common God. This was real Christianity. The kind you actually read about in the Bible. Radical encounters where God sends a messenger with a wild and life changing message. There really was no way to lessen the intensity of such an event. The words that would be exchanged from such encounters were always life changing. That is if they were actually given the importance they were due. These prophetic words were birthed in the Throne Room of Heaven. They were spoken thoughts of the Creator Himself. An all knowing and all loving being with an absolute knowledge of everything. Mere words from Him were as powerful to our soul as a tidal wave, a powerful and fast moving wall of water furiously clearing a naturally beautiful sea shore from all man made debris. Any time God had spoken to me it always seemed like a rushing wind would ravage my soul and leave behind the clearest of spiritual skies inside me. I quickly prepared for such an event as I could see Dave was about to speak. To my amazement all he actually said was that he could hear the Father laughing over me with joy. What a great thing to be spoken over my life. I was so happy in that very moment. I began to cry. The fact God was even paying any attention at all to my simple life down here on corrupted planet Earth overwhelmed me. The fact I had any capacity to affect His emotional status was beyond my wildest dreams. I sat there basking in the peaceful and awesome feelings of that moment awaiting for any other words to be birthed from Dave.

The silence that was no longer awkward continued for a few minutes, after which a simple dialogue began to unfold as Dave and I exchanged our stories of how exactly we had become entangled with God. He shared with me that he had been a minister since his 20s. He had been a speaker many times at powerful spiritual gatherings across the United States. But now in his later years he was called by the Lord to seclude himself in a house he built in the middle of the woods in Kansas. He went on to tell me that God had specifically directed him to come and speak to me and my wife. His initial hesitance to obey was based on many years of such encounters leading to him being rejected by the people he was sent to. Sometimes this would happen right away. Other times varying levels of relationships had been established between them only to later result in a hurtful spiritual break-up. Dave expressed though, that God was very stern and unyielding when it came to this directive involving me and Danielle. We went on to exchange phone numbers and after an hour or so of spiritual dialogue began the trek back to Michigan.

Chapter 30: Receiving the Next Step in Fulfilling My High Call

My drive home was still about fourteen hours long, but it was ever so different than the one there. I had so much to process. I had met up with Bo again. I had participated in a colossal and life changing altar call. And now I had met this Dave guy. Quite the spiritual impactful weekend. I drove home that morning a different man. Not to mention I now had a wife that had received a tremendous level of spiritual freedom. The importance and power of that encounter radically changed her. Danielle and I processed what to do upon our arrival back home. We were kind of weirded out by the whole "witchcraft" thing. We decided right away not to tell the women leaders back home about this event with Dave pronouncing freedom from the hooks they supposedly placed in her back. We really did not know how to proceed with our relationship with them going forward. What a spiritual quandary.

"Was I still called to be under their wing?"

"What was I supposed to do now that I knew they were witch crafting my wife?""

I knew these questions and so many more now would require long talks with my Father.

As we arrived back home we decided to not go back to another home church meeting until we had absolute spiritual clarity on how to proceed with our walks. I prayed to God to direct my choices and my path. I anxiously awaited a response from Him. I knew that everything had now changed. I felt so different, in ways I did not even understand. I felt like I had grown spiritually as a result of all the thing I had just experienced. I wanted to keep growing at any cost. I did not want to lose any more time not growing and becoming spiritually stagnant. I felt like my time with the two girls had run its course, but I did not know how to move on. I really did not even know if God would allow me to. I was so uncomfortable debating with them the directives I believed I had received from the Lord. So many forks in the road. So many choices that were made in fear of them attacking my faith-based obedience to my King. I felt like all of that would now come to an end. Unfortunately, I knew it would not be a smooth process. Even more troubling to me was I did not know what to do next. Where would I go to church if not at the house church? We spent a few weeks at the large Pentecostal church where my wife was Spirit filled. We even thought about joining it as members. All this somehow, though, felt wrong so we held back. One of my patients invited Danielle and I to her church. This invitation had been offered many times before but after continual declining on my part the invitations had stopped. I had felt before like I would be betraying the two girls by attending a different church. This was something that had unfortunately been programmed in me from early in my walk. So many churches claim they are only ones with the "real truth". Warning upon warnings to not attend any other church. Directives intent on displacing any desire to branch out in the body of Christ imposing a mandate of spiritual loyalty. Well, that day I felt free to open myself up for more options. I gratefully accepted her invitation and wrote down the address and directions to her church. I told her I was not sure when we would attend, but that we would soon. It was two weeks later that we decided to finally go to that new church. I remember driving into the parking lot of the large strip mall. It seemed to be an unconventional venue for a church. Then again I had spent the last year having "church" in the basement of a small suburban house. More paradigms that now needed to be shattered. I exited the car and began to make my way to the front door of that new church. I could hear the car lock in the otherwise silence in that lot on that early Sunday morning. As the door opened I could feel the sweet sounds of worship music pouring out. We entered to find the congregation engaged in the act of intense worship. The song playing I will never forget: "Prepare the Way" by Terry MacAlmon.

What a powerful song. I had chills overtake me as I could feel an intense presence of God filling that room. I was undone there in that new place surrounded by strangers. I felt so lost, but at the same time I knew I had actually been found. My God did not leave me in the state I was prior to the trip to Kansas. He had directed me there. I knew this was His doing. I knew that my life was now on His agenda more than ever. Nothing going forward in my existence would be meaningless ever again. My life was now God's, and to an even greater level than before.

We took our seats in the middle of the pack of Christians and closed our eyes allowing the presence of God to calm our spirits, and began to worship. I felt like a scared little kid in a big new school. I thanked God again for allowing me the privilege of being with Him on this quest for His Kingdom to manifest on earth like in Heaven. I sang from a thankful heart that morning. I wanted with everything I was to be someone that did exactly what that song said: "To prepare the way of the Lord." I held my wife's hand and melted away in the bliss of the love offered me by her and my Father. I felt so complete in that very moment. My ship had finally set anchor at a shore of peace. I cried again overcome by God's faithfulness to not leave me where I was, but to rescue me yet again. I could have spent the rest of my days there singing and thanking God for all He had already done for me. And it was in that moment that He decided to show me again in the most awesome way that He was still my Father and that I was still very much His son.

I could feel the presence of someone behind Danielle and I. I did not dare open my eyes. I could discern that whatever was about to happen was by the leading of my Father. His presence around me was overwhelming. I felt as if I had been inserted into a cocoon knitted by His very hand. I knew something was about to happen. Something spiritually monumental in my walk. Before I could even ask God what He was about to do, I felt a large and powerful hand grip my shoulder. I could feel a subtle shaking occurring within this person. I knew that they also were being overcome by the presence of the Lord and the holiness of that event. I was so yielded to my Creator in that moment, so broken before Him. I was wounded and felt so alone in my walk here in Michigan. I just wanted to crawl up in His lap and cry. I wanted my Father to hold me and tell me that it was all going to be okay. I desperately needed His reassurance more than anything else. I felt like such a little child there in the middle of it all. His silent comfort only elicited more tears to flow. I could feel love infusing into me from the hand that now increased its grip on me. My eyes remained closed and I raised my hands to my Father to acknowledge His doing in all this. Those human hands were nothing more than a means for the hands of my Father to reach out and comfort me. I knew it was Him there in the midst of strangers using a human vessel to offer my soul severely needed encouragement. I finally began to hear sounds radiating from the man behind me. I opened my eyes to see that the head pastor had made his way into the crowd during the worship and had positioned himself directly behind the two of us. He began to expel powerful words. Prophecy was the event now overtaking this holy exchange. I could discern God all over him and the words he would come to speak:

"The Lord says that He has brought you here to receive the next step in your walk to fulfill your high call."

I quieted myself and collapsed into the emotional cocoon around me. I cried thankful tears to God. I knew that I was still on His path for my life.

And I knew I was still His. My next step of this wild journey was about to begin. Little did I know how much crazier it was all about to really get.

Preview to Book 2

Let me tell you another climatic moment in my walk that was the spark that began a long process to saturate me in a supernatural and spiritual understanding of grace. It was a midweek day. I was back in Michigan with my wife, it was in the morning hours while she was still preciously sleeping. I was alone sitting on my couch in the living room praying and reading the Bible when the Lord spoke something to me super clearly:
"There were two trees in the garden, son."

I paused. I had become quite accustomed to hearing His words, but the tone with which he spoke those words that morning to me was very different. Like an innocent child I asked him: "What garden, Lord?"

I began to dialogue with Him:

"Do you mean the Garden of Eden?"

"I knew there was a tree there that Adam was not supposed to eat from, and after he did he was thrown out of the Garden for doing it."

"There was another tree there, Lord?"

I waited for an answer, but did not receive one immediately. I impatiently went in to the bedroom to wake up my wife. I was so curious and overtaken by the statement made to me by God that I needed to have an answer as to why He said it. I knew that my wife (unlike me) had spent some time in church prior to actually getting born again. I figured between the two of us she would have a better chance at knowing anything about this other tree. With a gentle and curious shake I awakened my precious wife. Her groggy eyes opened to a zealous husband looking down on her.

"Honey, what was the other tree in the Garden of Eden? I know there was the tree with the bad fruit on it, but there was another one, do you know anything about it?"

My wife responded as loving and gentle as any wife shaken awake from her sleep and being interrogated with a bizarre question could. She went on to tell me that she really did not know about any second tree in the Garden of Eden. I returned somewhat defeated to the living room. I was not going to give in yet. I was determined to find out all about this other tree. The funny thing about all this as I look back is the fact that I had a Bible right there with me. If I had thought of it I could have opened to the Book of Genesis and I'm sure that I would have found the answer there. But for some reason at that time I did not think of it. That question enveloped all my thoughts that morning. I prayed to the Lord for an answer over and over but no clear response occurred. Then finally I received an unction to go to a Christian bookstore ten minutes from my house. Not quite the answer I was expecting to my fervent prayer. I was not even sure it had anything to do with what I was praying about, I just knew that I had to go there. My now awakened and coffee bearing wife was told about what I thought I was supposed to do, and we left for the bookstore.

As we arrived I did not know what to expect. I was prepared for almost anything. Including a man standing at the door with the answer for me. After all that is how most of my days had become. I was constantly caught up in the supernatural life of the Kingdom of God. We entered the store and I paused. I asked the Lord why I was there. His answer again was not verbal, at least I did not perceive it that way. No, instead I felt another unction to go to a certain bookrack and to kneel down to look at the lowest shelf of books on that rack. I felt somehow like my body was moved by invisible strings by God, which was a great feeling to me. My eyes began to excitedly scan the books not having any idea what I was looking for. I knew though, that whenever I found what I had been sent for I would know in an instant. Surely, as expected, there it happened. My scanning gaze had come across a book that could not be regarded as coincidence; there it was right in the middle of all the other books hidden away: "There Were Two Trees in the Garden" by Rick Joyner.

This is where I will now share one of the dumbness periods of my walk with God, in hopes that it will encourage all of you when your time of spiritual non-genius happens.

www.ingramcontent.com/pod-product-compliance
Lightning Source LLC
Chambersburg PA
CBHW031404250626
47155CB00004B/1400

9780997012613